The King of Next Week

For Kathenne, thanks for sharing the magic!

The King of
Next Week

by E. C. Ambrose

Eee /E.C.
et. al
Reader con 7/10/23

GUARDBRIDGE BOOKS
ST ANDREWS, SCOTLAND

Published by Guardbridge Books,
St Andrews, Fife, United Kingdom.

http://guardbridgebooks.co.uk

The King of Next Week

ISBN: 978-1-911486-46-6

For the people of Malaga Island,
whose stories partially inspired this one.

CHAPTER ONE
June 1866

RAIN AND WIND LASHED the schooner *Diana* as she heeled into the gale. Waves crashed against the hull, but these waves felt different, a subtle change that resonated through the deck and the lines. Land was near, deflecting the water. With a surge of excitement, Captain Matthew Percy leaned far out from the rail, right hand clenched to the netting, left hand clasping his Union cap to his head. A safety line dug into his waist, the other end pegged near the bowsprit as the *Diana* heaved upward over a wave and crashed down again on the other side, adding a needless shower of ocean to the soaking he'd already earned. Lightning snapped through the sky. His skin tingled, the hairs on his arms standing. For a moment, Matt held his breath, suspended between the bucking ship and the lightning's veil of fire.

In that flare of brilliant light, he saw the island that shouldn't be there. "Land ho! Hard a starboard! Ready all hands!" he shouted, his voice already hoarse. Again, the ship heaved beneath him, and he absorbed the impact with bent knees.

"There is no land anywhere near, Cap'n!" the purser, John Crowley, hollered back. The pitching sea tossed Crowley against the rail like a soldier caught by a cannon's blast. "You've seen the chart!"

"Oh, there's land," muttered Tahari, the pilot they'd picked up at Tenerife. He crouched at the rail near Matt's feet, staring outward, oblivious to the rain. "Demon-haunted land. Spirits to drive you mad."

"He's already mad!" Crowley shouted.

Matt turned about, riding the tossing ship as if she were a wild mare and he were determined to tame her. "Will! Hard a starboard! Ready with the sea anchor."

"Aye, Captain!" His first mate's voice boomed through the rain. His grin flashed like lightning across his dark face. "Crowley! Back to work."

Crowley glared, but he obeyed, pulling himself along the lines back to the waiting crew. Crowley objected to the cargo, to the season, but most of all, to serving under a Negro mate. Matt had half a mind to bind the purser to the sea anchor and chuck him overboard. But Crowley was Lee's man, and besides, he needed all hands if he would harness the gale. If they could get to leeward of the island, it might offer some shelter, at least. If not, they'd be half-way 'round the Horn before they could get their bearings. On the other hand, he heard the Indies had a strong market for ice.

When the swells rose, Matt caught another glimpse of that land, closer now, a twin-peaked rise maybe as long as the whole of Phippsburg. The wind rushed them on, and he clung to his cap all the more. Stupid, to be wearing it on a day like this, but the damn thing had brought him through the War. Pray God it carried him through the storm. Rain lashed down his neck, red hair curled limp against his cheeks, but he dare not spare his grip to push it back.

"Should be me, up there," Tahari said.

"And you'd guide us to the demon isle? I don't think so." The point of land rushed toward them in a series of flashes, though none so powerful as the one that had dazzled him a few moments ago. With each stroke of lightning, Matt expected to hear the crack of a mast, but the jagged strokes struck upon the island's peak, making him wonder if Tahari might have the right of it. Demon-haunted. Matt had demons to spare, thanks to the War. They did not scare him anymore. Besides, who had more need of ice than a people who lived, so it was said, in fire. Over his shoulder Matt called, "Ready!"

"Aye!" Will roared back.

With each flash, Matt counted. Thunder rolled across the sky over head. Another flash. There! "Now!" He swept the hat from his head and waved his arm. "Will, do it now!"

"Heave! Heave!" Will ran down the deck and back again, an extra set of hands as the crew lifted the wood and sailcloth sea anchor and hurled it over the rail. The rope groaned against the capstan. Matt held his breath, praying it would hold. Then with the sharp grace that defined her, the ship swung about, her bow aimed along the island's sheltered side. A ridge of stone rose up like those formidable clouds that heralded the storm, then the mountain sheared into the wind, cliffs towering too close. *Diana* swept alongside the stone, blessedly slowing. The storm still battered him, but the wind died to a frustrated howl. He had dared the storm and won.

His shoulder aching with remembered pain, Matt unbent his fingers, not releasing his grip, but stretching out his hand, his muscles throbbing. How long had he been hanging on? He allowed himself a long breath as his men, his ship, his cargo slipped behind the island to safety. Again, the water changed beneath him, then *Diana* shuddered to a halt with the gritty sound of a sandbar deep below. Thrown off-balance, Matt snatched for the netting, but his numb fingers failed him, and he tumbled from the rail into the sea. Water sucked him down as he plunged toward the sand. By the distant flash of lightning, he saw a wash of gleaming red in the sand beneath him, crimson glass, apparently swept from the shores above and hoarded by the waves. He struck the sand, and his breath rushed into darkness.

***

A woman gazed down on him, her face glowing faintly, leaving a ripple in the air as she moved her head, an afterimage as if he had gazed too long at the sun. Her skin looked by turns darker than teak or mahogany, then swirled with ruby, reminding him of blown glass still moving in a smoky furnace. Her eyes flickered like a forge's light, her gaze arrested by something near his head, and her lips parted in a breath of wonder. His heart fell, wishing it were his face that captured her, but still, she smiled, and that was enough.

"What are you dreaming?" Will's voice.

Matt kept his eyes closed, heat pouring down on him from that distant beauty. Very well, it was the sun that warmed him not some glowing maiden with long, dark hair and flaming eyes. His head and arm throbbed, then a soothing cold settled against his skin, hands pressing the hard chill to his shoulder. Ice, to cool his fever. "Ooh, that's good. Thank you, Nurse Barton."

Will's laughter echoed around him. Somewhere

close by, water tumbled, and waves stroked a gentle shore. "You're not in the Morris Island hospital, Cap'n, and I'm no Clara Barton."

"More's the pity." Matt cracked open one eye. "I'm not dead then?"

"Not this time." Will sat back with a wince of his own, rubbing his back. He had a long face, deep-set eyes, and dense, curly hair no wind could ruffle. Overhead, a makeshift structure of planks, branches, and foreign leaves kept the sun from burning Matt a shade to match his own hair.

His mouth and nostril stung with salt. "You reeled me in?"

"Like a codfish, and twice as floppy. You ever thought about being short?" Will held his hand palm down, as if he could press Matt into a more compact form.

"Sure, I thought of it. Then I thought, when I get back to Phippsburg, Old Man Lee's bound to cut me down to size." He moved to sit up and pain swept through from his right shoulder, so he sagged back again to the blanket-covered sand.

"I keep hoping he'll give up on that." Will moved to sit beside Matt in the shade. He mopped sweat from his brow with a square of gingham so worn that the red checks were a uniform pale gold.

"Don't count on it." They shared a look that finished the conversation. *If you hadn't insisted on hiring me and those other Negroes,* Will would say, *your folk'd be perfectly happy to have you around.*

If we would've both died with Colonel Shaw, I wouldn't've felt the need, Matt would reply.

After the 54th led the charge on Fort Wagner, Matt found Will still alive in the press of the dead and dying. Before the assault, the rebels vowed to bury the white officers and the Negro soldiers together in a common grave, and with the Union retreat, everyone knew the rebels would bloody well make good on their oath. Will and Matt had limped out of that nightmare together. They wouldn't have made it as far as the field hospital without each other, and Matt was not about to let go now. "What's our disposition?"

Will straightened up and squared his shoulders to something like military bearing, in spite of his torn uniform and weary features. "Good and stuck, sir. Work's begun on repairing the topsails, and fitting the new rear mast"—the one that had gone down in the first violent assault of the storm as they rushed to reef the sails—"and some minor repairs. Three crewmen injured: Parker with a broken leg, McCobb, caught a splinter as long as your arm, and yourself, knock to the head, and popped your shoulder."

The usual: the damned injury that wouldn't let him be. Matt traced the sling on his right arm with his left hand, then followed it up to where a lump of ice wrapped in cloth sat cooling the ache. "You popped it back?"

"Wasn't so easy this time." Will gazed out toward the ship. "Crowley's got a bad case of the grumbles, and Tahari's been in the aft cabin since we beached, muttering about demons."

"We've already got one—Crowley. Who's the idiot brought him on board?"

"That'd be you, sir."

"Did you just call your captain an idiot?"

"No, sir, I just don't like to contradict my commander." Will grinned.

"Shut up." The entire crew, top to bottom, comprised the most motley assembly of sailors in all of Maine, the only ones willing to sign on to Matt's dream: in spite of Frederic Tudor's success down in Massachusetts a few years back, many sailors still held that a cargo of ice would melt en route, sinking the boat from the inside out. Aside from Lee, every shipyard in Phippsburg turned him down, all the faster when he explained his plan to have a mostly Negro crew to ship to the African coast. Matt held the bundle of ice to his shoulder and pushed toward sitting. Will caught him about the shoulders and got him steady.

Diana sat upright across a sandbar at the base of a stream that ran down from the forested slope behind. The three-masted schooner with her high prow and smooth lines remained the most beautiful ship he'd ever seen. Lee was a bastard, but he had some fine shipwrights. Aside from the upper mast, she looked awfully good for what she'd been through. Three injuries in a gale, and one of those was the same injury over again. Well, he could hardly count that. "Good and stuck, you said?"

"Look at her keel, how deep she's mired. Even the tide didn't lift her. I don't know how we'll get her afloat again, except…" Will shrugged. He rubbed his bit of gingham between his fingers.

"Except we unload the cargo. How much of it?" They looked at the ship together, shallow water lapping at her planks while the crew worked on deck or on the shingle nearby. Matt needed no reply, he could see the answer just by looking at her: too much. "Let's hope the demons need ice."

"Beg your pardon?" Will reached over and gently prodded Matt's temple. "Yep, knocked on the head, sure 'nough. I'm surprised that hard skull of yours didn't knock right through the hull and sink us yourself."

"I'm a madman—you knew that before you ever came to Phippsburg."

Will nodded. "Me, I'm resting up and making nice with the nurses, you, you're playing with your ice pack and dreaming of cold cash."

"Everybody flirts with nurses, Will—but they marry the rich ones. Where's Tahari? Tell him to get the demons out here."

"Dreamer." Will snorted. "You've always been the King of Next Week."

"I dreamed us this far, didn't I?"

Will took a leisurely look around, from the endless sea before them, to the grounded ship and the restless crew. "Oh, yeah, you sure did."

"Lots of folks'd be happy to live in a place like this—sunshine, fresh water, an ocean full of fish."

"And twenty-six men who ain't seen a woman for months. Sure, Captain. Keep on dreaming."

He thought of the woman in his latest dream and smiled. "Don't mind if I do. In the meantime, Tahari's our local pilot. Get him and the charts out here. No sense worrying over how to float her until we get that mast up. Meantime, I'd like to know where we are."

"Aye, Captain." Will rose to his feet. He reached back to his waist and pulled out something blue and streaked with pale salt. "You might want this." He chucked the cap to land neatly in Matt's lap. "The hat's lucky—dunno that it's done much for you or your head." He pointed, pinning Matt with his stare. "You take care of that arm, right?"

"Will do, Nurse Barton."

Waving this away, Will trudged back to the ship. Crowley stepped aside for him, a little further than simple rank required. They'd fought a war to free his people, to assure that no man could ever come north to claim his flesh—how long would it be before the rest of America gave up fighting? Matt's shoulder ached, and his fingers grew cold from supporting the ice. With a bit of fidgeting, he tucked the bundle of ice chips under the sling and reached for a flask waiting nearby—trust Will to think of everything. A few of the men stood out on the point to his left, hauling in nets full of fish that flashed in the sun. Just about paradise, this was, save that there'd never be a winter to deck the world in silence, nor an Autumn to make it blaze with color. After a little while, the slim figure of Tahari, a chart and a navigator's case under his arm, walked out.

"Captain, the mate says you asked for me."

Matt gestured toward the outspread blanket. "Join me."

Tahari gave a single nod, then settled awkwardly to the ground and lay the chart before him, but Matt touched the back of his hand—freckled finger to the tanned skin of the islander—and the man stilled. "What is it you wish, Captain?"

"We're not on that chart, are we. You and I both studied it before the storm hit, before we even set out."

The pilot's face crumpled. "We were meant to go north-north-east, sir, to pass into the Mediterranean. But the storm." He gave a little shrug.

"Aye, the storm. How far did we blow?"

Tahari looked down at the unopened chart. "Two hundred miles or more, Captain. Due south."

"Cape Verde?"

"Not so far, that would be a thousand miles."

"In between then. When the stars come out, we'll know more."

That precise nod.

"And you don't want to talk about where we are because you think you already know."

The man's shoulders rose, giving him the look of a vulture.

"Tell me about your demons."

"I am a Christian man, Captain." Tahari crossed himself just as precisely. "I do not believe in superstition."

"You did last night." Matt took another long swallow of the whiskey. "I hired you on, Tahari, I came to you because I know you've spoken of lands the other pilots don't sail to, people that other captains avoid. People who'd maybe be eager for trade with somebody who didn't mind who they are."

Tahari's shoulders slumped. "I know why you hired me, Sir, and yet I hoped you would not ask me to fulfill this commission." He waved to the island around them. "The people of Tenerife, they say the Lord made more things than Man. Three peoples, He made. Man, from the earth; angels, from the air; and, djinn—demons— from the fire, and it is the djinn who live here, on an island between the worlds."

"Dijon? Isn't that in France?"

"Djinn, Captain," the pilot corrected firmly. "They have powers, sorcery. They can change form and travel anywhere in a moment. They will grant three wishes, but they make a game of a man's desires." His gaze flitted about as if he were afraid they had been overheard.

The spark of inspiration struck and Matt brightened. "Genies, you mean? Like in *Aladdin and the Magic Lamp*. I saw a production in Boston before the war."

"This is a play for children—it is not the truth. Djinn are like any of us, they can be good or evil, faithful or cruel as they choose, but we have the power only of ourselves, and the Djinn, they have power over many things." He fell silent, staring at the sea.

Matt took this in, Tahari's sincerity ringing in his words. "When you mentioned demons back at Tenerife, I thought you just meant folk of a different kind, living in a hot climate."

Tahari blinked at him. "And that is why you brought us in this direction? Djinn are not merely folk. They are eternal and easily bored. They will taunt you, letting you think you have what you want, but they will fool you in the end."

A warning—or a call to adventure? For certain it wasn't a story he'd've heard back in Maine, much less a story he'd be living. At the shoreline beyond, one of the fishermen scooped into the net with both hands and pulled up a large fish shaped like a platter and sparkling in vivid blue and orange. "What in God's name is that?" Matt leaned forward, squinting at it.

"It is a parrotfish, Captain. I believe that is dinner."

Thinking of the silver-gray fish back home, Matt shook his head. The parrotfish looked more like silk than supper. "I hope it tastes as good as it looks."

***

That night, Matt devoured a double helping of roasted fish alongside a roaring bonfire on the beach, imagining he could taste the shining blue and orange of its scales. His misfit crew laughed and cheered, and he shared a wink with Will—who had re-stocked their ration of rum before leaving Tenerife. Back home, even on ship-board, they maintained a seaman's version of proper table manners. Out here, on the shore of their unnamed island, every man was a jester and a king. Sparks leapt into the sky to mingle with the distant stars. Matt wiped off his left hand—his right arm remained in its sling—and walked away from the fire, up to the headland above the *Diana*'s sandy berth. He had gambled on a trip to an unknown land, a place where ice would bring a thrill—and a high price—and he had lost. He crossed the stream and clambered carefully up, one-handed. Up here, far from the fire and the rowdy men, he let his eyes adjust to the darkness and searched the stars overhead to take his bearings.

"What do you seek?"

Matt jerked and turned at the sound of the voice, a feminine purr just at the edge of hearing. She stood at the edge of the stone outcrop, wearing a long garment that flowed and flickered around her, the stars faintly visible through the cloth, as if they were stitched into her raiment like beads. Rounded hips, long hair that rippled in the wind, her face invisible in the darkness. His mouth went dry, and he swallowed hard. "I'm always looking for something more, something new." He wet his lips. "Something unlike anything I've seen before. My father used to say I have a restless heart."

"A restless heart," she breathed, and her eyes kindled. "As do I."

"Do you, live here? On the island?"

"It is in our domain." She gave a regal dip of her head. She spoke with a faint accent he could not place—not Caribbean, nor European, nothing like Will's hints of the South and Africa.

A place between the worlds, Tahari had told him. Excitement drummed in his heart. "If we've trespassed, I hope you will forgive me. Our ship ran aground in the storm—we just need to make some repairs, and we'll be off again, I assure you." He glanced around again, able to see more of the island from here, stony outcrops and ridges among dense, unfamiliar trees. The same view he'd had by day when he came up higher, and not a clearing in sight. "We didn't notice any signs of habitation."

"We do not live as others live." She walked toward him slow and graceful as a cougar. "I think you know that. You know what people we are." She smelled of spice and smoke and heat, like the hearths of Tenerife. "You thought to sell us your cargo, did you not? I heard you speak of this and more." She circled around him, her breath warming his neck. "I have not seen hair like yours before—are you, too, made of fire?"

Just at that moment, Matt was hard-pressed to answer. Made of fire, oh, yes. She stepped once more in front of him, her eyes gleaming. "Do you not think, if we wanted your cargo, we might simply take it?"

Djinn. Demons. God's third race. He had no doubt she could take whatever she wanted. He wet his lips. But they didn't call him the King of Next Week for sitting around mending nets while other men plied the waves. Matt found his smile. "Well, then, if you like it, you'd never be able to get more. I'm guessing your people don't have much experience cutting ice."

"Ice." She elongated the word. "This is the thing you held earlier?" Her hand waved over his shoulder like a hot breeze, trailed by wisps of flame.

By the light that shone within her, he saw the face he beheld in his dream, and he nodded, his own face warming. "Follow me, I'll show you." He pivoted away, a moment of army precision, and one he hoped would give him a little more control over himself. His loins ached and his head swam with the scent of her. Was she, even now, working some magic over him? He needn't look back to see if she followed, her movement whispered behind him, and her warmth spread across his back and shoulders. He held himself straighter in spite of his injuries. He stumbled a bit at the base of the rock, where it met the sand, and turned back then. "Watch yourself." He put out his hand to the lady, by instinct, but she stepped down beside him, glancing at his hand as if it puzzled her as she strolled past.

Where her feet met the sand, it sizzled faintly, and she left shimmering impressions of her own bare feet. He knelt and stroked his finger over one of them—glass, still warm. Hurrying to catch up with her, Matt said, "You won't, that is, my ship is highly flammable, and my men will be right angry if it burns."

"And you? How should you be?"

Their eyes met. In that look, he saw his ship burning, his dream of owning it—and his promise to its master—gone in flames around a scorched heap of ice blocks piled in the shape of the hold, slowly melting into the sand. And himself, stuck here forever. With her. Either fate held attractions and dangers. "My name is Matthew Percy, captain of the schooner *Diana*, out of Phippsburg, Maine, and I should be pleased to welcome you aboard. I'm sure a lady of your discernment knows how best to manage herself."

Her smile glinted with a flash of her teeth. "Indeed, Captain Matthew Percy. You may call me Janiri." She drew a deep breath and let it out in a sigh no warmer than his own as he showed her to the ramp that led up to the deck.

They crossed among rigging and spars, tools and materials laid out for work to begin again next morning, He brought her to the hatch and propped it open, taking a lantern down into the hold. Janiri stumbled a bit on the ladder, with a chuckle of delight; a creature of fire, magic, and joy. Ducking below decks so as not to jar his head, Matt hooked the lantern above the next hatch, then knelt down and slid it open. She knelt as well, leaning into the cool breeze that arose from the opening. Beneath its insulating sawdust, most of the ice lay invisible, but Will had swept clean a block half the size of a bench and chipped off part of it for the good of the injured men. The block gleamed pale blue, its faceted corner edged in white and reflecting the lantern's glow into tiny shards of light that danced around the hold. It glowed like the new snow of winter and washed over his skin with the promise of skating, ice-boating, the creak of ice breaking up on the Kennebec's shores, icicles of maple sap dripping from the branch tips as the first warning of spring.

"Can you feel it?" he whispered.

Janiri leaned in closer, holding back her hair with one hand, her skin warm, her eyes closed as she breathed in the ice. "It is delicious." Her lips curved, and her eyes barely opened, watching him like a cat. "This is a wonder such as I have never seen. Do you have other such wonders in the distant land of Maine?"

He grinned. "Maine's about as different from here as a place could be." He tipped his head toward the ice. "Do you like it?"

She leaned in, mist curling around her face as she sighed. "I believe we should like this cargo very much. We will send a delegation tomorrow evening to negotiate."

"And you?" His voice felt too husky, no longer his own. "What should you like?"

Her hand stroked across his brow, sliding back the tumble of his hair. Her fingers trailed down along his beard and rested lightly at the corner of his mouth. He dare not breathe as she traced his lips, his chin, the pale, bare stretch of his throat where his pulse leapt against his skin. "Oh," she murmured, "I think you know that, too."

Her hand lingered at his throat as he said, "Is it true you can grant wishes?"

"Only three—one for each of God's peoples. A wish is the union of the wisher's desire, and the djinn's spark, their power. Many things my spark may deliver, but I cannot give them all."

He imagined her in the flowers of a New England spring, among the leaves of autumn and delighting in the swirl of snowflakes like stars upon the air. Dancing in his arms at a ball up at the mansion, lying beside him to warm a winter's night. "I wish you would come home with me, as my wife."

The ice below echoed with Janiri's laughter. "You needn't have wished for that. My people have free will, just as yours do." Then her face grew somber. "But if I choose you, you must know that I cannot stay forever. I am not of your world of ice and earth and ocean, but I am curious. As you say, a restless heart."

He had expected more ceremony, some magical tingling that sealed the wish, but her laughter was enough for him. "Stay for as long as you can," he answered, then, "for as long as you wish." The word blew a breath of longing to mingle with the mist of the ice and the lantern's fire.

"I will come home with you, Matthew Percy, and be your wife." Flame kindled beneath Janiri's skin, and she glowed.

***

Beneath the blazing tropical sky, Matt stood sweating in his blue wool coat, brass buttons gleaming, his shoulder aching a little, but out of its sling in any case. When the sun touched the ocean, she had said, and it sank a little lower by the moment. In the meantime, he prowled like a caged cat. Will stood by, likewise dressed in his full uniform, tracking Matt with his eyes. "Might's well be at ease, Captain," he murmured as Matt paced by.

The other crewmen muttered restlessly, and he caught bits of their conversation. "—no island on the chart, no habitation, surely—" Tahari.

"—fucking lunatic—" Crowley.

"—get home sooner, maybe 'fore the birth—" Joe Darling, a Malaga islander with a pregnant wife back home. Matt smiled faintly, imagining his own new wife. If she didn't turn out to be a mirage, some fevered imagining. God, what a fool he'd look then, making the crew dress and stand at attention, making them wait for a customer who'd never arrive. Tahari watched him darkly and did not speak. Matt's heart fluttered, his palms sweatier than the rest of him. She would come. She must come.

Will started whistling, low, and sweet, one of those spiritual songs they used instead of hymns. Down the line, another of the men started singing, very softly. He glanced up the line toward Matt, who gave him a nod of encouragement, and the man broke out, full voice, as if they stood not on a beach on an unknown shore, but in the aisles of the finest church in Boston.

Mustering the 54th, the enlisted men sometimes sang like that, a rare beauty the officers weren't meant to know about, much less to approve of. Their commander, Colonel Shaw, strongly discouraged them from fraternizing with the men. By the time they reached the beach at Fort Wagner, fraternizing had resumed some of its original meaning, for how could a man face enemy fire without seeing his companions as his brothers? Matt gazed out to sea where the sun's red glow reminded him of the burning fort, flames lighting the way for the rebels to gun them down. He stood on the sand thousands of miles from South Carolina, suddenly rushed with fear as if this would be another debacle, another beachhead of utter chaos and disaster. His men, fractious at best, would never listen to him again if the buyers never came. Mutiny? Perhaps even that. Would the Negroes stand with him, or would their camaraderie as sailors supersede their discipline?

A splash of blood glinted in the sand. Matt jerked as if he'd heard the blast and felt once more the stabbing fire of a musket shot. He caught his breath and rubbed at his eyes. When he looked down, the blood remained, and Matt stalked closer. An imprint of a slender foot, formed of glass, reflected the sinking sun. He recalled the red glass in the sand beneath the waves and imagined her pacing on the beach of an evening, at the urging of her restless heart. He let his breath out slow and released his left hand where it had instinctively risen to support his right elbow. She was real, whatever that meant to someone like her. He squatted and traced the footprint, smooth and cool, his fingers casting a dark shadow that interrupted the blood-red sun.

Will's whistle rose to a summons, and Matt pivoted on his heel. Through a break in the trees, a young man with skin the color of burnt clay appeared and stood aside, holding a fluttering banner of purple edged in gold. The crew stopped their muttering and stood straight, their song dying away. Into that silence rose a trill of music. A pair of flute-players stepped from the trees, followed by a man who wore a round-bottomed drum on a band across his shoulders. He beat a sinuous rhythm as he led forth a delegation of men. They wore loose, flowing trousers in vivid hues edged with golden threads and long tunics with slits up to the hip. Sharp black beards and crisply curled dark hair framed many faces, though some were clean-shaven and others completely bald. Eight men in all, each of them as tall as Matt himself, and a few even taller than that. The man who walked at their head wore his hair down past his shoulders, pinned back on one side with a jeweled comb.

Matt's parched throat for a moment released neither breath nor sound. The delegation stopped mid-way along the phalanx of sailors. The second stranger, smaller, though small only by comparison, flicked his glance along the crew. The leader stared directly at Matt, who drew himself up as if he were greeting Colonel Shaw at parade, and strode up. He restrained himself from saluting, but instead gave a tip of his head. Damn, he should have asked Janiri about protocol and manners, anything he should or should not do when the delegation arrived. This moment was either the boldest moment of his life, or the most foolish. Quite possibly both bound into one.

"You are Captain Matthew Percy," said the leader.

"I am. And whom do I have the pleasure to address?"

The leader stepped gracefully aside and held out his hand, bowing at the waist to present the man beside him. "May I introduce Shamhurish, the King of Thursday."

Behind him, Matt caught the smothered hiccup of Will's laughter. Before he could frame a prayer that the delegation hadn't noticed, the King of Thursday cocked his head. "Why does this man laugh?" His eyes flickered with fire, his hands glowed gently.

How on Earth did he address such a being? My Lord? Your Majesty? No ordinary Yankee had acknowledged a king for almost a hundred years. "Sir," Matt said, "I ask your indulgence if my men seem indecorous. They have had a long voyage, and did not expect to host such august company."

Shamhurish gazed at Matt for the first time then, his lashes impossibly long and thick, his eyes rich and warm. He was, without doubt, the handsomest man Matt had ever laid eyes upon, the kind of man that made him question his own predilections. "And yet, the others stand silent and still, as you have no doubt instructed them. This one did not. If it is necessary to correct his fault, our negotiations can wait."

Oh, shit. Was he meant to? For a fleeting moment, Matt wondered if the only way to impress these people would be to instill obedience in his underlings, to treat his men in whatever wicked fashion the demons would. As if Will were his underling, and not his friend. He hardened his stance. If he would not bow to a foreign king, then he would not bow to their idea of discipline either. If it cost him the contract, so be it. "Sir, among ourselves, a moment of humor is no fault at all. On the contrary, it is often a tool we use to bring two parties such as ours closer to an accord. May I introduce First Mate William Johnson." Matt gestured Will up beside him, where his friend gave a short bow. They shared a glance.

"Beg pardon, sir," said Will, "It's only Matt—Captain Percy. Sometimes we call him 'the King of Next Week'.

Didn't expect we'd meet another such monarch out here on the ocean, sir." He gave that half-bow again, then stood with military precision at Matt's side, a solid presence to ground this moment outside Matt's own daydreams.

At that, Shamhurish studied Matt again, and the hints of fire receded. "Indeed. Then we are well-met." He put out his hand.

Matt pictured the sand fused to glass beneath Janiri's feet, and his blood felt cold, then he clasped the hand of the king, cool and unyielding.

Shamhurish held his grip a long moment, then gave a nod. "I grant your petition of marriage for my daughter. A feast shall be laid and the marriage consummated this night."

The twilight shifted around them as if a hundred shadows danced among so many flames. Eight men there had been, hadn't there? Matt brought his attention back to the king, Janiri's father. Good Lord, a princess of demons. What had he truly gotten himself into? Sure as fire, there weren't any girls back home like her. "Thank you, sir. I will endeavor to be a good husband to her."

"Yes," said Shamhurish, a sheen of mist rose from their hands, "you will."

"My lord, we should inspect the cargo," said the king's, what, bodyguard? First-mate.

Shamhurish released Matt's hand, and smiled, showing no teeth.

"Sir, I've had my men bring out a sample for your examination." Matt showed the way, and Shamhurish and his mate strolled forward, their cut leather slippers making no different impression in the sand than the feet of other men. The dance of shadow and light beyond the forest distracted him, but Matt turned to follow, and Will fell in step beside him.

"Marriage?" he mouthed.

Matt nodded, then flashed a grin, and answered, "Consummated tonight."

Will laughed without sound and cuffed his shoulder. Beneath a canopy next to the ship, two crewmen presided over a table moved out from the mess. It bore a cloth-wrapped block of ice misting gently in the glow of twilight and the two lanterns set on poles beside it. His cargo master, freeman Jed Tripp, reached forward and peeled back the cloth with grave attention. Beneath lay a pure block of Phippsburg pond ice, a foot thick, two feet long, a foot and a half wide, its edges just beginning to soften. It gleamed faintly blue within its frozen heart and reflected shimmering light back to the faces of the two djinn as they stood over it. The mate squatted down, staring into the block of ice, catching a drip on his palm where it skittered and sizzled as if dripped onto a griddle. He straightened quickly as if shocked and stepped aside, holding his fist closed around the drop, or the moment of its fall. Shamhurish raised his hand over the block, letting the mist swirl around his dark fingers. He waved them gently, and the mist spiraled and writhed around his hand. He breathed deeply in and blew out his breath into the cool air over the block.

For all the times Matt imagined the negotiation process, he never imagined something like this: a reverent, almost religious encounter between a man and a piece of ice. To a Yankee, ice came easy, growing of its own accord every winter, a surface for skating over or boating on, for breaking through to get to the fish below, or preserving in ice houses into the summer, for cooling drinks, impressing visitors, and that most sacred of all New England institutions, the making of ice cream. Damn—he wished he had a cow or two and he could show the djinn what ice was really good for. In the next moment, he realized he could: if he spoke that wish aloud, Janiri could fulfill it. A crazy waste of a limited resource. He'd have to think very carefully before using a single one. Matt held his tongue.

Shamhurish spread both hands over the ice, moving in gentle strokes as if he measured the block with the span of his hands and his arms, as if he could embrace it. "How many have you?"

"One thousand, two hundred seventy-five."

"May I pay you in emeralds?" The sleek darkness of Shamhurish's hair swung into the pale glow of the ice as he admired it.

Emeralds? Shit—he had no way to evaluate emeralds—he wasn't sure he'd ever seen one. Matt cleared his throat. "We can accept payment in gold, sir, if that suits you." At least he could bite-test gold, and melt it to check its purity.

Shamhurish straightened at last and glanced at him, then he waved a hand toward his mate who produced a thick gold coin from his pocket and held it out. "Five of these per block, and we shall take your entire cargo."

"May I?" He held out his palm, and the coin dropped into it, heavy and slightly warm. Matt examined the coin. It had to be at least a twenty-dollar piece. A hundred dollars a block—that was a hell of a lot of money. But it was also their first offer. He rolled the coin in his hand, flipped it into the air and let it drop back into his palm. "Ten." He said, offering the coin back. "And my men will unload them wherever you wish."

The king stared at him, his eyes kindling slow fire, crinkling slightly at the corners as if he held back his smile, and there Matt saw the echoes of his daughter's delight. "Ten." He tipped his hand. "I am sure another captain would not hold his stock so dear as to send his crew home empty-handed." He made a soft rumble at the back of his throat. "Six, perhaps—seven at a stretch, but ten?"

At his side, Will gave a little, strangled noise of his own. Matt, just this once, ignored him. "Suit yourself. You're our first prospect, sir, and I'd hate to sell short, especially given the chances of another captain even finding this place. If you don't want it." He signaled to the cargo master who took up the cloth and covered the glistening block. Before Tripp could grasp the other corner and conceal the ice completely, Shamhurish gave a sigh.

"Very well. Eight. And we shall unload them ourselves."

Matt smiled. "I can write up the contract."

Shamhurish waved this away. "Paper does not do well among our people." He arched an eyebrow and tipped his head toward the block of ice where a clear impression of his hand remained though he had never touched it. "But our exchange, too, can be completed tonight. Keep that as a surety. As my people unload our cargo, we shall likewise deliver the gold."

No contract. Unusual, but for the price he was getting? If they came through with the gold, then paper be damned. "We'll have to load the payment after the ship's afloat, sir, or I'm afraid we'll be outstaying our welcome." Sliding the coin into his watch pocket, Matt held out his hand. "Meantime, it's a pleasure doing business with you."

"Likewise." The two men shook, then the king enfolded Matt's hand within both of his. "Come, Captain, and let us feast. Bid your men accompany us."

"Will? Organize to have four men stay with the ship and supervise the transfer—we'll take it in shifts so nobody misses out."

"Very good, Cap'n." Will strode away, barking orders as Matt accompanied his new customers back toward the forest.

"Captain?" Tahari came up and gave a sharp salute. "I will stay here as well, for all of the shifts. I am, ah, I will be more comfortable here." His glance flicked to one after another of the djinn, and his eyes edged with white.

"You'd be welcome, Tahari, but do what you must." He returned the salute, and the pilot hurried away. A ripple of amusement spread through the djinn.

"You and he alone recognize us," Shamhurish murmured. "It is well this way. These others...they should not know, or it may go ill for them. Their memory of tonight will be indistinct."

"Understood, sir," Matt replied.

Preceded by the drum and flutes as before, they walked the path into the forest. When the ship first grounded on the sandbar, while Matt recovered from his injuries, a small party of men had ventured into the trees to ascertain any resources or dangers it might conceal, but they had not crossed the saddle of land that rose between the island's two peaks. Nor had they mentioned a well-trod path between the trees, and he wondered what they made of it now. The sand readily gave way to rough gravel and a thicket of tall green stalks with huge cones of flowers. More flowers burst from every tree, upturned beckoning cups of white, pink and gold like a china cabinet come to life. Tiny birds flitted among them, scattering as the men approached, swishing and diving through the air to the tree canopy above. He saw a few palm trees, but more tall, twining, broad-leaved trees sheltering green fruits the size of apples. Lizards rushed from the path, tails flicking into the deep shadow. The trail mounted upward, and Matt soon felt the weight of the woolen coat and shirt beneath. He tugged at his collar, envying the practical loose garments of their hosts.

At the top of the saddle, they broke free of the trees to gaze down into a soft bowl of terraced land spread with pink, gold, and white pavilions, rippling cloth embellished with rich embroidery, arranged into courtyards. Deep-dyed rugs with patterns of leaves and flowers to match the forest itself spread between the tents and along the shore where huge fires crackled. A broad stone breakwater continued the bowl of land, providing shelter for a half-dozen ships with high prows and triangular lateen sails. Someone behind him breathed an oath. Had all of this been here the whole time they camped on the beach and ate parrotfish? Matt feared that, if he touched one of the tents, he would find it wasn't there at all. He kept his hands to himself as they descended stone steps toward the harbor.

"This is not all of our people, of course, merely an… outpost?" Shamhurish explained.

"It's beautiful, sir." Matt gazed in wonder all around him. Real or illusion, he spoke the truth.

"I am gratified by your enjoyment."

The gathering of crimson, green, and purple at the harbor's edge resolved into lines of women, richly dressed, and Janiri stood at their head. "Welcome, sailors from distant Maine. Come and share our bounty." She spoke to all, but her gaze lit upon him and did not leave.

"Cap'n?" Will said. "You want me to oversee the crew that's coming to unload?" He alone stared back in the direction they'd come, his face lit by the hundred torches mounted at the pavilions around them.

"I want you to relax and enjoy a night off, Will. And to meet my wife." He gripped his friend's shoulder and steered him around. As they turned, Janiri stood there, an arm's length away, crowned with a cascade of tiny gems that twinkled like stars in the midnight of her hair. Both men caught their breath, then Matt said, "William Johnson, who served with me in the recent war, meet Janiri, daughter of Shamhurish, the King of Thursday."

Will took her strong hand atop his palm and bowed over it as if he might kiss it. "Pleased to meet you, ma'am."

"And I, you." The warmth in her eyes as she looked on his friend made Matt's heart swell. She kept Will's hand. "Come then, and dance."

"I don't—" Will began, and she laughed.

"Of course you shall! Come, come." She took each of them by the hand and skipped toward a broad courtyard where musicians gathered, beating drums, blowing on flutes and sawing madly with bows across instruments with far too many strings. Janiri plunged them into the rings of dancers. Men formed one circle, women another, the two circles moving through each other as women danced beneath the arms of the men, careful not to touch them, the two rings cycling against each other, the pressure of nearly meeting made palpable at the places where it seemed they must touch. The men laughed and caught Will's hands, drawing him in, and a few other sailors with him. He continued to protest, but they had already danced away, the man beside him shouting instruction for the sequence of steps.

"What about me?" Matt asked, but Janiri did not release his hand. Instead, she clasped them both and drew him with her beneath the joined hands of the women's ring until they stood at its center.

"Women and men do not dance together, save only on their wedding night." She moved side to side, her feet still bare, still gliding beneath the fall of her wrapped skirts. He matched her movements, steps to one side, a step back crossing over, steps forward again as they circled each other.

"Only then?" His eyes drank in her every sway. Every moment living with her would be like opening a new volume in a library of wonders. "In Maine, we can dance together any time we want, once we're married. But we don't dance at arm's length." He lifted their hands, encompassing a circle of their own.

"No? How is it dancing in Maine?"

"Like this." He shook free his left hand and pulled her close, guiding her free hand to his upper arm. "Here, hold tight. Keep your arm strong, then you'll feel which way I move, so we can move together. I go forward, you go back. Sometimes you spin." Then he slid his hand across her bare back, folds of silk brushing his skin, his fingers stroking across her skin, feeling the shift of her muscles as she moved. Her lips parted, her face now mere inches from his.

A whoop of excitement rose from the dancers around them—gales of laughter from the djinn, and howls of delight from his men.

"Maine is a nation of barbarians. I shall try to fit in." She gazed up into his eyes as she mirrored his steps, following his lead instinctively. "Am I doing well?"

His voice felt thick, his loins aching. "Very well."

Her lips curved into a smile, and she cocked her head. "Your eyes are green as emerald—I have never seen such eyes before."

"I wonder if we'll have green-eyed babies," he answered, and she laughed again. The sound danced inside of him like the flame inside a lighthouse, reflected by a thousand facets into a brilliance that would call him home.

Janiri leaned in close and whispered, "Let us find out."

***

After slipping out of the circle of women, and through the circle of men, they danced away from the crowd in a series of waltz steps, turns, and promenades. A large gathering sat on richly patterned rugs laid along the stone patios as servants passed bowls and platters of steaming delights—but Matt had no interest in such things, not yet. Shamhurish raised a silver goblet to them as they danced past.

"Is all of this real? Is any of it?"

"Of course it is, but we do not usually entertain on such a scale. We live between the worlds, and we can draw things from there to here. From a single bone, we can make a meal. Was any of this here last night? No, not a tent nor a torch nor a rug. Here, look!" She broke the grip of his right hand. They had come to the end of the curved harbor where another set of steps led upward into a grove of almond trees. A lone tent waited in the sweet almond breeze, its flaps tied open and a brazier glowing within. He started to move in that direction, but Janiri remained where she was, and he followed her gaze.

On a dais of sand, gleaming beneath the stars, rose a dome of ice. The blocks stacked atop each other, offset like bricks in a wall, bowed out and rising up to tower above them. An opening showed pale blue in the night. A penumbra of mist enveloped the ice dome, as if it, too, were unreal. And yet it seemed the only real thing around, aside from his own flesh and blood. He walked toward the dome and they stepped inside. Faint lights from outside lent the dome a bluish glow and the temperature inside fell sharply. Janiri let out a sigh that misted the air. "Is it not beautiful?" She let go his arm and danced a slow circle around him, letting her fingers trail along the ice. Where she touched, faint lines appeared, a spiraling pattern like strange writing. She stood out in pale red like a rising dawn against the chill gleam of the ice, and Matt shivered. Already his nose and fingertips tingled with the cold that she embraced.

Janiri tossed back her head and laughed, the sound echoing in the tinkle of the gems at her forehead. "Ah, Matthew, let us take you someplace warmer." She caught up his hand and tugged him back outside to the balmy night.

"That can't be all the ice," Matt said, resisting her direction to stroll around the dome instead.

"No—this is only the first. I am sure Father is already considering how best to enjoy his treasure."

They came back around to the base of the long stairs, and Matt gave the dome a last admiring glance. "And they built it so fast."

"Too fast," grumbled a voice behind him, and Matt spun about, setting Janiri a little behind him.

Crowley leaned against a stone pillar at the start of the jetty, aiming the cup in his fist toward the dome of ice. "That there, that ain't natural." He shook his head. "Not a'tall. How'd they do it? Starting to think that Tahari's got the right of it, and we here have been dealing with demons. How else'd they get it done so fast?"

Matt relaxed, but only a little. "I imagine they were eager to unload. All these little boats and a strong crew." He shrugged. "I've been dancing and rather let time get away from me. Once they brought it over, I imagine they simply stacked it up as they desired."

"Won't last long this way, will it? It'll melt in a day or two, come sunrise."

"Well, then, we'll have to come back and sell them more. You should stay with the others—that feast smells exquisite. Better than parrotfish anyhow."

Crowley pushed off from his post and swayed a step nearer. "But their women are something, ain't they, Cap'n?" He pushed his mug toward Janiri, whose warmth rose steadily at Matt's shoulder. "How'd you get so lucky? Fuckin' madman like you, how'd you get the luck?"

Matt stiffened. "I like to think my boldness pays off from time to time."

"Gonna keep 'er to yourself on the voyage home, or do we get a share of that, too?" His eyes gleamed liquid and shot with red.

"You are a very rude man," said Janiri.

The heat of her itched at Matt's side, and he took a half-step forward, as much to gain a little distance as to enforce his own position with his crewman. "The lady is correct. And the lady is my wife, Crowley. Go back to the others. Whatever you've been drinking hasn't helped your manners."

"Right. Aye, Cap'n. Go find my own, I will. Some other darkie—" Crowley attempted a salute, but nearly toppled into the harbor below. Matt lunged forward and grabbed his arm, hauling him further from the water.

The thought flashed through his mind that he should've let the bastard fall—maybe the shock would sober him up. But, thanks to Lee, the man was his purser, and he owed some responsibility even to an ass like Crowley. Sighing, he looked to his wife. "I'm afraid something'll happen to him if he tries to get back on his own. I should—"

"Very well," she said, her voice hot and cutting, "They

will make sure of him, and you need not worry."

Two large men emerged from the darkness where no one had been before. More magic? A sharp, hot breeze murmured around him like strange voices, and the two men nodded. They looked more than adequate to the task of wrangling a drunken seaman. Matt let them take hold of Crowley.

"Matt, come. We have other business."

That was the truth. He re-joined Janiri, and the stroke of her hand down his arm distracted from his other concerns. She stood one step above him, her hands gliding along his arms, up to cradle his face, tipping his chin so she could kiss him, light and hot. He stepped up into her embrace, and she kissed him again, longer this time, leaving a hint of smoke on his tongue. Together, they ran up the steps, leaving the harbor far behind. The curtain door rippled shut when they ducked inside the tent, keeping them close and safe from the rest of the world. "We should be gone when the moon rises," she whispered. "All of this, it is hard, even for my people to keep such a dream alive. Your men must be back to the ship."

"Then we shouldn't waste time." He fumbled with the top button of his coat, and she ran her fingers down his chest, the buttons sliding open one after another until the coat rustled to the thick rugs at his feet. His cravat unwound and fluttered away as if carried by unseen hands, then the mother-of-pearl buttons on his shirt began to tug free. "Slow down there," he said, tapping a finger against the button over his heart.

"Now who is wasting time?" she asked.

Matt shook his head and moved in closer. "You're

used to everything being fast and easy, but some things are worth lingering over. Besides," he brushed his fingertips among the gems that rested across her forehead, "It's not enough to be naked. I want to feel you." The gems winked as he disturbed them, and her eyes flashed as well. "To feel you touching me. Me touching you."

She reached between them and toyed with a button, then slid it free, her hand brushing against the hairs of his chest. Janiri made a little sound of interest, sliding her fingers beneath his shirt. "Red as fire."

"Where I come from, some think that hair makes me a demon."

"Only because they know no better. They are, indeed, barbarians."

"We're all of us barbarians once in a while."

Lowering her head, she parted the v of his shirt and pressed her lips to his chest, just over his heart. He gasped at the sudden flare of heat, and his knees trembled.

He slipped aside his braces as they sank down together, her lips on his chest, the hollow of his collar bone, his throat. His hands found the end of her intricately wrapped bodice and gave a gentle tug. Laughing, she rolled away, letting the silk unwind, baring her breasts. A pin of gold and pearl clasped the skirt, and he pricked his thumb as he worked it free, a drop of blood shimmering. She took her hand in his, caressing his palm, bringing his thumb up to her mouth, her tongue sliding over the injury. He groaned.

Janiri rose to her knees, shifting her hips one way and the other, shimmying her skirt down to pool around them. When the buttons of his pants slipped loose of their own accord, Matt kept any protest to himself. He couldn't wait much longer. Her knees braced to either side of him. She rose over him, his hand still clasped in hers, her tongue sliding over his thumb, their bodies sliding together in a moment of fire. They rocked their hips, and she moaned, her head tipped back, gemstones twinkling. Her hair tumbled down her bare back, down all the way to his thighs, stroking him as they moved.

Janiri's skin glowed, her veins like dark ribbons of smoke tracing every beat of her heart. Fire licked up within her. The vessel of her form bound an inferno, and he could feel her restraint as the heat rushed through them both. When he set his hands upon her hips, his skin sizzled, and he pulled them back, lying beneath her. With every shudder of her flesh she pulsed with flames. If she but released herself completely, he would, in an instant, be turned to ash and blown away in the breath of her desire. Their sweat rose up in steaming tendrils, wreathing her until they cried out together, and her flame roared to life above him, a towering pyre that took his breath away, and just as quickly, gave it back again.

The rush of fire died away, the brazier dying with it and plunging him into darkness. The sound of their paired breathing and the quiver of her gemstones echoed the peace of the union. His heart still thundered, his sweat gone instantly to steam. In the darkness, her hand stroked through his hair. Her fingers traced the line of his collar bone, then down, shivering the skin along his side, to rest upon the puckered flesh of the gunshot wound that nearly killed him. She traced her fingers back again, following the scar where a bayonet sliced across his chest, then skimming the line of his jaw back to touch the corner of his eye. She sank down, her chest pressed against him. He hesitated a moment, then slipped his singed fingertips across her hips and back, her hair silken against his skin. He lay beneath her utterly spent, suspended in the night as full of gratitude as she had been full of fire. If he would have her to wife, he must expect to get a little burned. His arms encompassed her completely: only because she chose it, because their union, for whatever reasons, gave her joy, and he was pleased, and proud, and just a little terrified that he had been the one to share it.

A pale, rising light illuminated the walls of the tent, casting the embroidered patterns into lines of shadow. The moon rose, and Matt's heart sank, only to rise again. This was no end for them, but only the beginning.

"Yes," she whispered against his face, her fingers tangled into his hair. "Yes, we must go." He pulled her even tighter, feeling every inch of her against him, then let his hands fall. She lay still a moment later, then peeled away from him, and finally rose, reaching down to draw him up with her. Her silken wraps languorously drifted from the floor and slid up along her legs to clasp at her hips. She held out her arms as the second piece whispered around her, folding in the air as carefully as any maidservant might do, her breasts wrapped once again, her hair settling into smooth waves along her back.

Matt chuckled as he worked his way into his own socks and underthings. He found his trousers and tugged them on, pulled his rumpled shirt over his arms. His right shoulder twinged a little, but not so much that he couldn't stand it. Slowly, he buttoned up, replaced his bracers, smoothed out the shirt as best he could—but no man would have any illusions as to what his captain had been doing. Let them know it, let every man see, Matt Percy was in love, and such a woman he brought home to wife. Crowley's comments of the evening came back to him, and he knew that for every man who envied him his bride, another would disdain him for the choice. It grew so wearisome, these divisions among people. He had been made of earth, and she of fire—what of it?

Janiri stood by the entrance as the curtains furled back and tied themselves, letting the moonlight drape her in silver. She turned back, her features lost in the curious light. "Something troubles you."

He buttoned his cuffs, replaced his lucky hat—very lucky indeed—and dangled his jacket over his shoulder. No need for that just yet, as he came to join her at the door. "Some of my people, back home, they won't view you kindly. They are too much concerned about the color of a person's skin."

"And yet you sail a crew of many shades."

"I do, by my own choice—I had to fight the owner to hire so many Negroes. Plenty of folks think you get more than two or three on a crew, and it's asking for trouble. My parents were what we call abolitionists—they wanted to do away with the enslavement of Negroes by whites. We fought a war to make it so, and my father died for it. I almost did as well." She reached out to touch the bullet scar, and he nodded. "Not everyone believes in the cause, nor thinks the war well-fought. They want to keep the wealth of the South in the Union, but they'd rather the Negroes stayed there, enslaved to a wage at the very same work. Those folks might not look too kindly on you."

"I can be of any shade I choose." She stepped away into the light and her skin grew pale, her eyes and hair still dark as she looked back at him.

"No," he said forcefully. "Don't choose this for the small-minded men you've not even met. You are made of fire, Janiri, you're not beholden to any of them."

Her skin bloomed once more into its gold-brown tones, deepening with a sheen of red, and she smiled. "No, I am not, and I am pleased to see that nor are you. Let us go meet them together."

They walked down the steps hand in hand. In the round valley below, nothing remained but the half-burned cookfires and the gleaming dome of ice with a trail of glass-bound footprints leading in and out and all around. Matt smiled to see them, imagining Janiri's people reveling in the novelty of their icy cave. What would they do with the rest? Raise a palace, or maybe a temple? Lay down their fiery heads upon pillows of ice and feel its chill caress them to sleep?

"Can we go inside one more time?"

He tugged in that direction, but she said, "No, Matthew, I think we should not." Her gaze danced in that direction, then away.

The light of the moon draped the dome in silver, shining against it, and through it. Something distorted the far wall. Matt's uncertainty returned, but Janiri still did not look at him. He broke her grip and walked the few paces to where the ice dome stood misting beneath the moon like its earth-bound reflection.

The tracery of hundreds of trailing fingers marked the outside of the dome, sometimes forming intricate patterns like those of the rugs that cradled their love-making, but the markings traced much higher than any man could reach. Hand-prints, smoothed by the heat of their creation, clustered around the entrance, an impermanent sign of the owners that echoed the glassy footprints down below. And inside.

Matt stopped abruptly, his breath caught. Several feet off the ground, in the wall opposite the doorway, John Crowley hung embedded in ice, his spread arms encased in icy bonds, his knees bent to lock his feet against the wall. His neck arched back so that his head sank to the mouth in the ice. Janiri's own light as she came to stand at Matt's side showed Crowley's eyes wide open behind the ice, his mouth gaping. Blue-lipped, skin several shades too pale except where frost shaded it black.

Nausea clutched his gut, but Matt refused to turn away. "You knew about this."

"Not this precisely. He was a bad man, unworthy of your crew. He deserved punishment—it was not I who determined what form that should take."

"Not you? Your father, then?" Matt's fists knotted, and his right shoulder throbbed with the tension. "He deserved some discipline, yes, but not to lose his life, not just for being an ass."

For a moment she made no reply. "If my people overstepped, then I am sorry." Her voice, for once, held no hint of warmth.

Overstepped—they had melted the ice around him,

imprisoning him. How long had it taken him to die like that, gasping for breath or screaming for aid? The feathery pattern around the dead man resolved into the prints of a hundred hands pressed into the ice around him, outlining his tortured body, and down below on the sandy floor, so many glass footprints that they formed a pool reflecting the horror up above, as if they had been dancing around him while he died.

"Take him down! Get him down from there. My God." Matt stumbled forward to clutch at Crowley's chest. His hands stung with the cold. Ice cracked around the embedded arms and feet, then finally around the buried face and the body thumped hard into Matt's arms. He staggered with the cold, solid weight, forced to let Crowley's blackened feet drag along the ground out of the dome of ice, where he laid him on his back. Matt knelt there, gasping for breath, then Janiri's shadow joined him.

"We are not like you, Matt. We are not made of flesh, and there are many things I am sure we do not understand." She sounded curious, a little sad, perhaps.

"We don't kill out of hand, Janiri. And we don't allow those who depend upon us to die without need." He pressed the back of a shaky hand to his mouth. While he had been uphill, making love with his wife, Crowley had been shoved into the ice, dying, a spectacle for all of her people to see, his corpse hanging like a gruesome decoration in their treasured cave of ice. Like a crucifix in a temple of demons. "Thou shalt not kill—how hard is that to understand?"

His breath caught as if he carried a bullet lodged this time in his chest. His body shook, flashes of memory bursting like cannon shot behind his eyes: a man gutted and flopping to his death at the end of Matt's bayonet, the smashed remains of the 54th scattered on the beach, the dead and dying men he clawed his way through to find Will, to find their way home. He reached out and tried to shut the dead man's eyes, but the lids froze open, making his eyes too round, shriveled by his frigid death. Matt spoke very low. "If I wished for it, Janiri, could you bring him back to life?"

She knelt beside him, matching his quiet tone. "I cannot. There is none upon this earth who can." She touched his shoulder gently. "If I were able to, would you wish it?"

He blinked fiercely. "Indeed I would. No man should die like this, and to lose a member of my crew to the family of my bride? Janiri, I don't even know what to say. I know he insulted you, and me as well. No doubt he'd've done it again, but this—" He broke off, swallowing hard.

Her voice sank to a breath, and she asked him, "Do you still wish for me?"

Matt bowed his head, fighting to master the visceral responses of his flesh. He was a man of earth, after all, and given to all the strength and weakness that came of such an origin. He had dared to take a bride from the people of fire. Tahari warned that they were demons, that no magic came without a price. Finally, he raised his head and met her eye. She had never yet looked so serious, contrition and worry pinching her brow. Did he still wish for her? After such a night of fire, he wanted her even more. Had he paid with Crowley's life to win her?

"You are thinking very hard," she said.

Matt gave a nod. "My mind is troubled, but my heart says yes."

"Then we shall see what can be done to ease your mind." She smiled, but only a little, to his eye, the perfect amount to acknowledge both her relief and his concern. By God, he was a madman, and in love.

CHAPTER TWO
September, 1866

THE RELIEF OF BEING HOME, surrounded by the thick green foliage of late summer, quickly gave way to fretting. Matt had sailed victoriously into the harbor at Parker's Head, to the cheering of sailor's wives and children. Lacking a purser to keep accounts, Matt paid the men from his coffers. After seeing to the proper berthing of *Diana*—the ship soon to be his own—he delivered his log and the money to Lee's representatives dockside. He shared a brief embrace with Will before he took Janiri home to the square-built house on the bluff where he had grown from boy to man. For the first few days, he barely left his bed, catching up on all the sleep of the four-month voyage, and enjoying the company of his wife. But as his exhaustion passed, along with the euphoria that followed, Matt presented himself at Lee's shipyard only to be turned away with a perfunctory order to wait for Lee's own message. Lee had only just returned home himself and needed time to process the records of the summer's trade, or so they said.

Three weeks passed before the summons arrived. Three weeks of waiting, only to have the interview explode in moments. Leather panels embossed with gold covered the walls of Lee's office, above oak wainscoting aged and brown. Matt felt he had crawled between the covers of some ancient tome written in a language he could no longer recognize.

"Mr. Percy." *Mr. Percy*, like an ordinary sailor, not *Captain Percy*, as it should be: no oversight for a man like Lee. "I see the gold. Indeed, it is hard to miss when one's sailors have been flooding the bank all month demanding their share be changed for cash they can actually spend." Old Man Lee sat behind his oaken desk, cold as a codfish and twice as slippery. He folded his hands together, his fingers thin as blades. "What I do not see is the contract you claim to have sealed with the family of your…" He cleared his throat, and his ears beneath a fringe of white hair looked a little pink. "Your wife. By their own account, the men were drunk when the deal was struck, and most of them have little recollection of overseeing the transfer of a thousand blocks of ice, much less of meeting those you claim have purchased it. They recall only rowing the boats full of gold back to the vessel after it regained the sea."

"Then where the blazes would I have gotten so much gold?" Matt demanded, shoving the pile toward Lee. A few coins tumbled from their stacks and winked upon the desk. "Sir. We stocked the rum when we reached Tenerife, and yes, the men might've been celebrating rather hard. Who wouldn't? We survived a gale, and made a success of the venture, in spite of everything. Our clients hosted a grand feast to honor both our trade and my marriage."

"Where would you have gotten the gold? Where indeed." Lee picked up one of the coins and rolled it through his palm. "At a guess, I would suppose piracy." He clasped the coin in his fist, veins showing beneath his papery skin.

"Piracy!" Matt erupted to his feet, slamming his fists on the desk that separated them. "For God's sake! You dare accuse me of piracy? Do you think the men were so drunk they didn't notice our boarding another vessel? Or had you not noticed the *Diana* carries no arms but what we need to defend ourselves!"

Lee's fishy mouth clamped upward, long lines drawn down from either side, then gave a twitch that might have been a smile. "You're right, of course, Mr. Percy. Burglary is much more probable. You and your Negro getting the men drunk, then off-loading the cargo and taking up arms against a local bank or merchant. There's no evidence you ever went further than the Canary Islands. Or perhaps you had previously stolen and stashed the gold, and bargained for this commission to retrieve your ill-gotten fortune and launder it into a ship to carry on your criminal behavior. Of course, by your own request, half of your crew were Negro, beholden to a man who paid so richly and had his own Negro at his side to vouchsafe their position."

"Will Johnson is a war hero, which is more than I can say for—" Matt broke off. The bastard only brought Will into this because he knew it would pitch Matt right over the edge. "Our logs show bearings for the length of the journey, including our layover at Janiri's port—"

"Which has no name, nor does it appear on any chart. And who is it who keeps the log, Captain?" Lee made an insult of the title. "You would not be the first to forge your own account of things to cover up your mis-deeds. Did John Crowley discover the truth of the venture, and is that why he died?"

"Are you adding murder to your accusations? He was

drunker than the rest, and in a foreign land. If you're saying we should have watched him more closely, that, I'll own—but the fact I lost a single man over the course of the journey hardly makes me a criminal." The gruesome corpse, bound in sailcloth, had been buried on the shoreline and marked with a cross. Drowning while drunk made a plausible tale for the other sailors, but the image of Crowley's ice-bound corpse joined the gallery of the dead that haunted Matt far too often whether night or day. His chest burned, his right shoulder throbbing. Lee was just like every smug commander he'd ever met, convinced that Matt was doomed to fail and determined to prove it. When Lee agreed to put up his vessel for the journey—a vessel he said Matt could take as his share of the proceeds—Matt barely believed he had convinced him. But the voyage was a rich man's gamble, a way for Lee, the ship-builder, to turn a greater profit if Matt's outlandish scheme paid off, selling a load of pond ice on the coast of Africa. And now that it had paid off most handsomely? Matt forced himself to sit back down, the leather seat squeaking a little. "Sir. Just as you say, there is no evidence I am lying. Are the men saying anything against me? Anything that would support a different version? Perhaps you'd like to speak with Janiri, I'm sure she would—"

Lee thrust up his palm. Now they came to it. "Mr. Percy. I would think, as a lifelong resident of Parker's Head, and the descendant of a fine line of Phippsburg residents, you might at least observe some decorum. Most captains, when they bring home a foreign strumpet, have the good sense to drop her and her offspring at Malaga and return to the fold with some semblance of piety."

"She is no strumpet, sir, she is my wife, lawfully wed, first by her own laws, and now by the Congregational church not a hundred yards from where we sit." He displayed the thin gold band cast from the coin her father had given him as surety. "I have no intention of setting her aside."

Lee's fingers folded back together. "Come now, Mr. Percy, we are gentleman, and tradesmen. Certainly I can understand a young man's desire to taste adventure with his first command. And having seen your woman, I believe the attraction is perfectly obvious. I am not unsympathetic to your base nature being roused to such a woman. You are not the first Yankee to develop a taste for the exotic, you shall hardly be the last. Having done so, however, most then return to sanity. This." he flicked a glance toward the gold. "The entire affair has put our town on edge. The sailors have gold they cannot spend, and at least one night they can barely recall. You have brought home a most inappropriate bride, whom you apparently think to settle in our own community. I knew you were bold when I agreed to this venture; that is why I thought it might succeed—and why you agreed to the contract you did."

"We both acknowledged the risk, sir," Matt replied, thinking of all the yards that turned him down.

"Indeed, however, I did not take you for a fool. I have agents on a vessel bound for Africa on a scientific study. At Tenerife, they will seek out this pilot you claim to have hired. They will investigate and return with such evidence as they are able to uncover, though alas this process will take some time, given the storm season rapidly approaching—" Matt opened his mouth and Lee wagged his head. "I accuse you of nothing, not yet. I merely let you understand that I have my suspicions. Should my agents turn up anything to support your claims, naturally, I will be pleased to stand corrected, and deliver my most humble apologies. In the meantime, I shall retain the gold against the possibility of it's being ill-gotten and in need of return to its rightful owner."

Matt's fury sank through him, weighing him down as Lee swept the gold back into the chest, one of twelve they carried home like kings. Brought to the shore by the same mystery that unloaded the ice as he and Janiri bound their lives together, and Crowley lost his forever. One last coin tumbled through the air to join its fellows. They shimmered with the promise of tomorrow as Lee slammed down the lid. Matt flinched at the sound. "Sir. What about the *Diana*? What about my ship?" His own voice sounded hollow with despair. The back of his throat burned.

"At least you have returned her in more or less usable condition. Our agreement, you may recall, depended upon your not merely trading the ice, but opening a new client to be supplied exclusively by my firm. You have no contract. You have no customer, not even a chart that shows where such a customer may be found for a second delivery. The agreement is void, Mr. Percy."

Nor would he ever again deliver ice to Janiri's people, not if they would put it to such use. Matt locked his fingers through his hair. "You can't leave me with nothing, sir." He felt as queasy as a cabin boy.

"Of course not," said Lee, his voice warming. He pushed a sheaf of paper toward Matt, who eagerly picked it up and scanned the lines, his momentary hope withering in the instant. *"Eight thousand, six hundred and twenty-seven coins of gold, nationality and origin unknown, received of Matthew Percy by Charles Lee, owner, as surety against the contract dated April 4, 1866, regarding the voyage of the Lee-built vessel, Diana, with a cargo of ice bound for coastal Africa, coinage to be held in escrow for one year, pending confirmation of delivery as claimed."* A receipt for the confiscated gold. And all he was likely to get from the bastard. No wonder he'd been comfortable with Janiri's father: it wasn't the first time he'd worked with a demon.

"If you'll just sign there, and here again, I've drawn up a copy for each of us. We are men of business and we mustn't neglect our paperwork."

With numb fingers, Matt signed, clenching the quill so it did not quaver in his grasp. He tossed it down and curled his copy into his hand, shoving it inside the inner pocket of his coat. Pushing back his chair, he collected his cap and rose. He hesitated, then pulled the cap onto his head and turned about to face Lee, but refusing to do so cap in hand. "Sir. I need to provide for my wife who is, as you have so crudely noted, expecting."

"Well. I cannot keep you on my rolls here, as I am sure you understand," Lee tapped his finger to his lips. "The sawmills are always hiring."

Matt raised his chin, freshly shaved for the occasion. "Sir, you trusted me with a ship, and a crew, and, with a sole exception, I brought them home safely—that's more than many a captain can say. I deserve more from you than your suspicions and your ink."

Lee's watery gaze regarded him for a long moment, then he flipped back the lid of the chest and counted out five coins, dropping them into a leather purse, which he held out by the strings. It swayed like a man on the gallows. "Don't forget to amend your copy of the receipt, Mr. Percy, to reflect the payment."

For a moment, heat pounded inside his skull and he wanted to grab that purse of gold and swing it like a weapon smack into the old man's face. Matt snatched the purse and slammed out the door before he gave in to his rage. Even as he left, he heard the scratching of quill on paper as Lee followed through with his paperwork.

***

On the steps, Matt forced himself to pause and slip the purse into his pocket, far from the record of its kindred thousands. Enough to buy the ship and more—enough to give Lee a royal profit on the venture, to pay him back amply for the outlay of supplies and the risk to the vessel itself. Thank God Matt had paid his own sailors, in spite of the trouble they'd had with gold coins in a town so small. Should've taken the lot up to Bath and made a deposit. He'd have to for his share. Five coins, worth…well, he had to admit he had no idea. A captain's wage for a four-month journey? Hardly. He pivoted on his heel and marched away from the Lee's four-square white house along the graveled street. From the shade of a maple in full summer's growth, Will rose to his feet and stepped to the street, pulling his hat back onto his head against the August sunshine.

"Did'ja hit him?"

"No, not for lack of wanting, though." Matt realized he'd been cradling his right elbow, a habit whenever his shoulder ached. Whenever he carried a bushel of worries that tightened every muscle. He released his grip and rubbed the back of his neck. Should've cut his hair shorter as well as shaved, but the thought of Janiri running her fingers through his hair made him leave it long.

"Matthew," Janiri breathed, striding down the street, a parasol propped on her shoulder. "Have you had your meeting, then?" She appeared, as she had that first day, from nowhere, and yet, as if she had been there the whole time, an effect that nobody seemed to notice but him. He found her a smile, though it felt slender and brief.

"Afternoon, Missus Percy," Will said, tipping his hat, then glancing at his watch, the one luxury he'd bought out of his own share.

"Don't let me keep you if you've got something better to do, but I thought you might like to hear how it all came out," Matt snapped.

"I am sure we both can see it ended poorly." She stopped in front of him, her calico dress still swaying a little in a breeze of her own making. Cotton, she pointed out, resisted flame. She loved ruffles, the way they tickled against her shoulders, framing her face, or against her wrists, and had cascades of them added to her gowns. Two, only, he paid for, one blue and one ivory with tiny flowers, but today she wore a green one. Did she wish them up for herself, or had she some other means? He had to talk with her again about restraining her sorcery before somebody noticed.

Will's brow furrowed, but he held his silence, clicking the watch open and closed.

"Just as well. Let's go home—I'd rather not speak of it in the street. Will—join us?" Matt took Janiri's hand over his arm and glanced back. He expected Will to fall in stride as he'd always done, but his friend hadn't moved.

"No, I've got…" He trailed off and rocked a little on his feet.

"Got dinner plans?" Matt suggested. He found a stronger smile. "Is it Miss Eliza Darling? I know she's been waiting for you."

"No woman ought to wait for me, Matt. I've said that before." The pocket watch slipped away, but his fingers remained in the pocket where he kept that bit of gingham.

Janiri's hand tightened on Matt's arm, and he covered it with his other hand, her heat rising through him. "Maybe she hadn't ought to, Will, but you can't deny that she is. She's a fine woman, for all that she's from Malaga, and I'm sure she'd—"

"Don't you be talking down Malaga. Those folks work harder than anybody hereabouts." Will's raised voice drew some stares, and one of the passing carpenters stopped short, turning their direction as if Matt might need his help to control the angry Negro.

"I'm sorry, Will, I know you're right," Matt replied softly.

"Someday, I should like to visit there. It sounds quite interesting," Janiri offered, and Matt squeezed her hand to let her know she'd gone too far—she didn't know much about the locals and their ways, and what she did know, she never understood quite the way she ought to. When they stepped out together, he navigated the twin poles of pride in his new fortunes, and fear lest she take offense and instigate another Crowley.

"Look, I do want to hear about the meeting, alright?" said Will. "Just, maybe later, down at the Bell and Anchor."

Matt shook his head. "No place public."

Will finally met his gaze. "That serious."

"I'll be looking for work down the sawmill tomorrow."

"Oh, Matt." Janiri drew closer to him. "You were not meant for such labor."

"It's what I have. It's what folks do around here when they've got no alternative. When they can't sail." He broke away from her grip. Shit.

Shit shit shit. Matt strode down the street, walking hard, wanting to run. A few ladies out for a stroll gave him nods, and one of the old sailors lounging on a bench binding the end of a rope hollered a greeting. Matt had nothing to say to any of them, not right now, not until he could trust his voice again. Anger curdled behind his breast into defeat.

When was the last time he cried? When his mother died? He'd been twelve years old, suddenly charged with caring for his two younger sisters in their father's absence, taking to the sea when they were old enough to be left. Ten years later, his father fell on the battlefield at Antietam, but Matt couldn't recall crying when he heard. How else should his father have wished to die, than in battle for a cause he believed in? Instead, Matt fostered Rebecca out to a good family in Bath, wrote a letter to Margaret down in Portsmouth where her husband worked in a foundry, and set off for Boston to enlist on his own. Maybe he wept for the pain of his arm the first time it dislocated, and the rifle shot that tore through his side, but that hardly qualified a man as a weakling. Come to think of it, he didn't recall seeing any tears streak the blood that caked Will's face for the pain of his own injuries.

Now tears burned at the back of his eyes and if he just moved fast enough, he'd out pace them for sure. When a man can't sail. Could he even do a lumberman's work, or would his weakness be revealed, his arm dangling, useless. No use explaining. They'd never regard him with the compassion reserved for soldiers who came home missing a limb. No sir, he looked as able-bodied as any man, and any words of his just made him out to be the liar that Lee evidently took him for. God damn Lee. Putting the shipyard behind him, Matt walked a little further, leaving the sound of the ocean behind as well. At least, as far from it as he ever could be on the jagged peninsula that was his home. Would this still feel like his home if he couldn't get out on the water? With Lee's suspicions, no other owner in Phippsburg would hire him, and the rumors would be flying across the island already. If he weren't already tainted by his friendship with Will, and now his marriage to Janiri, the rumor of piracy would ruin him.

Matt scrubbed his face with his hands. God, he wished he could...what? He stopped, his hair sifting down over his fingers. He still had two wishes, didn't he. Wishing for Janiri's hand in marriage seemed so frivolous in hindsight, but the impulse gripped him so hard, the desire and the mutual fascination he saw in her eyes. He could wish for Lee to have a change of heart. He could wish for a ship of his own, or the fortune to build one—imagine that, he and Will working together to build their own ship, maybe founding a shipyard. And yet.

Squaring his shoulders, Matt lifted his face and tugged his cap back into place, touching the stained gold braid that still wrapped it. In other regiments, the officers wore plain caps so they couldn't be targeted, but in the 54th, the officers, all white, stood out pretty clearly from their men in any case. Might as well wear it proudly. He'd fought his way through everything he had in his life, as hard as he'd ever fought on the battlefield. The idea of simply wishing up a change felt foreign. Two more wishes, and he must save them unless there was no other way forward.

Soft whistling reached him up the path, then Will strolled into view against the backdrop of dense forest that clung between stones. Will tipped his head, studying him. "You alright?"

"I will be. I don't know as you'll want to associate with me, though. Apparently, I'm a criminal—Lee just hasn't figured what kind."

Will whistled a falling note. He came up a few steps nearer. "Because you can't produce a contract? What an ass."

"Why didn't I think of it? I knew he was a bastard about paperwork."

"Guess you were a little distracted. Maybe you should've got some help with negotiating."

"I know, I know. Janiri's people, her father—they're

pretty reclusive. It's why their island isn't on the charts. They like to be left alone." Matt stopped himself before he embellished any further.

Will rocked a little on his heels. After a moment, he said, "You don't know all my secrets either."

"Will." Matt turned to his friend. "I don't mean for this to be a secret—sure as Hell I don't want it to come between us. I just—I know some things in confidence that I'm not at liberty to share, not even with you."

"Guess I'll just head over to Malaga where I belong. You get on home; your wife is waiting for you." He started down the slope toward Phippsburg's southern shore.

Will's rebuff stung like a slap in the face. After all they'd been through together, he had to know Matt didn't think that way. The anger he had buried since leaving Lee's office rushed back. "You don't like my wife, is that it? Are you just as prejudiced as the rest of them, or is it personal?"

At that, Will stopped. "Ain't nothing like that," he called back. "I told you, you don't know all my secrets. You got your own now, fine, you keep it."

Secrets again—what secret was Will keeping even closer than the lash marks that scored his back? He had every right to be angry about being left out of the talks to sell the ice, but Matt figured he'd get over that in time, especially given the money they'd brought home, money for ships, for marriage, for whatever dreams Will might possess. Except that Lee had confiscated all the coins not already paid out to the men, and Will's avoidance began long before they made port. He avoided Janiri for two months on the ship, and now at home. When he came calling, he stayed the shortest time possible, and since they announced her pregnancy, he hadn't come at all. If he didn't disdain her foreign origins, and he didn't dislike her personally, what could make a man forsake his best friend?

Matt saw his friend's back retreating. What did it matter the reason? Will walked on, picking up his pace, and Matt ran to catch up, clasping his shoulder.

"Will, don't be like this, please. I've already lost everything I've been working for, don't make me lose you, too."

Biting his lip, Will looked away, his work-hardened shoulder like iron under Matt's hand.

"You don't like Janiri, that's your right, but I am not giving up our friendship over that. We've been through too much already." Matt swallowed hard. "You keep your secret, I'll keep mine—just so you don't believe I'm the scoundrel Lee's making me out to be." He started to lift his hand, but Will's swung down and clamped on top of it, his dark eyes searching Matt's face.

"You're no liar, no matter what Lee thinks. Whatever happened back there, it's killing you, keeping it from me; I've seen that since we left the damned island. Whether Crowley drowned in his own piss or got hisself stabbed by the locals, I got no doubt he earned it." He sighed. "As for the other. You love her, she loves you. Got no room for me, and there shouldn't be. You got to make your own home, Captain. I ain't leaving you, I'm just telling you the truth. It's not we don't like each other, Janiri and me, it's just hard to see how to share you." He gave Matt's hand a gentle pat. "We'll figure it out."

Matt's jaw clenched, and he did not trust himself to speak. He nodded his thanks, rubbing the corner of his eye with his thumb.

"Besides, if I know you, by this time tomorrow, you'll be thinking what to do next."

"Sure. Sign on with the mills."

The men shared a smile, Will's as weary as Matt's expression felt. "Then I'll see you there." Will released him and gave a little salute as he set off down the trail. "Get on home! Don't keep her waiting."

That there was what made their friendship work: Matt was always working for tomorrow, and Will was always looking out for today. Between the two of them, they'd somehow be alright. He had to believe it.

***

As Matt walked home, sunset stoked the clouds with pink and gold reminding him of the vivid colors of Janiri's native clothes. How could he tell Will that, all the long voyage home, he'd been half-afraid the gold in those chests wasn't real? That he'd been dazzled by magic and beauty, and made a bargain with demons, a bargain Crowley bought in blood? Crowley, who froze to death on a tropical island. That the real treasure he carried were those last two wishes that festered at the back of his mind.

A grassy slope led from the road up to the house on the bluff, painted the cheerful blue of a summer day with cloud-white trim at the corners and sills, its two chimneys standing proud against the sky. Smoke unfurled from the easterly chimney, and Matt frowned. He scraped his boots on the metal ridge by the doorstep, then entered the smoky hall. "Janiri? Are you alright?" He waved away the smoke and hurried to open the damper on the kitchen flue. A fire roared in the broad hearth, and the metal spit bore the weight of a woodcock he'd shot a few days past. The oven stood open and smelled of bread, slightly burnt.

"Cooking is very difficult." Janiri stood by the thick slab of a table, a knife in one hand and a bundle of carrot tops in the other, their sorry green fronds splayed out against her arm. "These parts you do not eat, correct?"

Matt burst out laughing, and she glared at him, some of that fire entering her face.

"Do not laugh at me—I am trying to be a good wife. I am to cook, yes?" She hurled the handful of greens at him. "It was so much easier before. The same bone can make a meal over and over. Now I can barely find my way between the worlds." Her face creased, and she groaned, her arm pressed to her belly.

Matt lost his humor in an instant and hurried to her side. "What's the matter? Is it the baby?"

"Don't touch me." In a flicker of shadow she stood across the room, and the air swirled with heat, her voice still echoing in the room.

Hands spread, Matt stared at her. "I'm sorry."

"You don't even know what to be sorry for! Be my wife, you say, conceal your spark, you say, come to my home, you say! And here I am—for what?" She flung the knife across the room, but before he could even flinch, the blade exploded into a hundred shards that scattered across the table and floor to lie glinting in the firelight. "In my home, I can be whatever I choose. I can be wherever I choose. But here, every day I am hurt, I am sick, I am tired! This child, the earth and the fire war within me, and even to come to you as I did—the things I used to do exhaust me. And every day it is harder to be this and not that." She thrust her hand toward the hearth and flames burst from her skin, her translucent arm rippling with crimson power and streaks of shadow. "Your men stare at me, and your women will not speak to me except to ask if I, too, will burn in the sun. And I will burn, Matt, oh yes, I will."

She spread her arms, her gown shredding away as light and heat poured from her.

"Janiri, please don't! Please." He stumbled toward her and dropped to his knees. Then a thought struck though him with stinging clarity. "Have I done this to you? Did my wish imprison you?"

"Your wish. It was not your wish that brought me here, Matt, and I have said as much! You need not wish for this, I told you, I would give it willingly—it is not that which binds me." Her eyes glowed from a wreath of smoke, and his own eyes watered.

"What then? What binds you here if you want to go?" He stared up at her, thinking of God's chosen, lost in the desert and following the pillar of flame. Her brilliance hurt his eyes even as her pain broke his heart. "If you can't find happiness here, Janiri, go home. I would hate to lose you, but not so much as I hate to see you suffer."

"You have no joy here, either, look at you. Your own people cast you down, and yet—give me a wish, Matt, let me show them how we are to be treated."

Matt felt her burning, as if his own fury manifested before him. Confronting it like this, he searched for an answer. Why did he not give up? Why not compel

Lee to believe his story, or the people of Phippsburg to accept his wife? Because that, too, was a form of enslavement, and he would not have it. "I have joy," he said softly. "I have joy in you. I have joy in thinking of our child, growing inside of you. I take joy from Will's whistling and his friendship. Today, as I walked to the shipyard, an osprey flew overhead—you must have seen them—wings spread and white. Glorious. Outside, the leaves are turning, have you noticed?"

Her head turned, and he rose, beckoning her toward the door and flinging it open. She followed haltingly, the woman's form shifting and flickering within the fire. "Look. Autumn's coming. The leaves can't ever glow as bright as you, I know, but I wanted you to see them." He sprang down the steps and gestured toward the mouth of the river. "Wait until winter, when the ice comes. You saw the blocks I brought you, but they're nothing. They're so dull, just like bricks of cold." He shook away the image of Crowley's tomb. "Every one of those stones by the riverbank, they'll be rimmed with ice, like the ruffles on your gowns. Have you ever seen snowflakes? They're like lace made of ice—you're going to love them. And the springtime! Janiri, all these bushes are lilacs. They burst into blossom, purple and the smell is divine."

"I have seen lilacs in Persia," she said as her fire ebbed. "I did not know they could grow in such a place."

Standing in the glory of his home, before the glory of his wife, he said, "The question is, can you?"

The shreds of her gown gathered up around her, clothing her nakedness as the fire sank back within her. "I do not know. You told me I would be noticed, and not in the way of admiration." She stepped down from the granite stoop and stood beside him, gazing at the lilac bushes as if she could see the blossoms. "It is hard to be so alone. You have been… Distant."

"I was waiting on Lee, for all the good it did me, but that dream's over with now." His left hand cupped his right elbow, then her hand settled on his shoulder and the warmth sent comfort deep into his bones. "I'll think of something. I'm the King of Next Week, after all."

"What does this mean, 'the King of Next Week'? You are not a king as my father is."

"Dear Lord, I hope you didn't expect—"

She smiled at him. "No, Matt, I could see you are not of that kind."

His anxiety softened. "Will came up with it. In the fishing communities around here, the best fisherman is known as the king of the town. Me, I'm always fishing for something bigger, something that hasn't come yet."

"The best at fishing for the future."

"I'm not the best at anything, but I don't let that stop me." His smile felt crooked and worn. Lee's insinuations swirled inside, and among them, a curious grain of truth. "There's a place, Janiri, where you might not feel so alone. Get your shawl. I'll pack up that bird."

Together, they crossed the rough spine of Phippsburg and borrowed a boat. His coat left behind, in his shirt and braces, Matt rowed them across the short span of water. By the time they reached the island, a handful of children clustered near the overturned boats, children with faces dark and light and every shade between.

"Jonah! James! You get back up here and finish your chores!" A young woman emerged from the fringe of woodlands, a baby's head just cresting over the wrapped shawl across her chest. She stopped short. "Why Captain Percy, what brings you over here?"

Matt turned to give Janiri a hand out of the boat and pulled it a little further on shore. Looking at the dark-skinned woman, Janiri asked, "Is this Malaga, about which I have heard so much?"

Matt nodded. The very place where Lee told him to dump his foreign whore. The one place he knew where white and black mingled on the land, and in the families.

"Susan—how's the baby?"

"He's fine, Cap'n." She grinned and rolled back the cloth so they could see the child's sleeping face. Janiri made a little sound and walked closer, scattering the children back among the small houses. "And we're that glad you got Joe home in time for the birth—it was a near thing, I tell you that!"

"He is beautiful." Janiri stared down into the child's scrunched face, a few curls of dark hair marking his brow.

"Thank you, ma'am." Susan's glance flitted between them uncertainly. "Are you here for Joe? Or is it Will you're wanting?"

Matt shrugged. "Actually, I was looking for you or Eliza." He slid his arm around Janiri's waist. "Things being what they are, Susan, we can't afford to hire help."

"Sorry t'hear that, Captain." The baby wriggled, and Janiri gasped with a hint of that delight Matt remembered. Susan began a swaying motion, that hypnotic tool of mothers the world over.

"My wife needs to learn how to cook."

Susan burst out laughing. "I expect a fine lady like

you's never cooked a thing, am I right, ma'am?"

Janiri drew a breath, and heat rose against his skin. "Shhh," he murmured close to her ear. "That's the truth, Susan. I'm happy to share from our garden or the hunting, whatever I can, if you can help."

She glanced toward the mainland. "You don't think this'll be more trouble for you, sir? I'd hate to see that happen. This ain't no place for a sea captain, or his lady."

"I'm no sea captain now, Susan," he began, but Janiri said, "I am not beholden to small-minded men."

Susan put up her chin. "Come along, ma'am. I'm about to put on the griddlecakes." Over her shoulder, she hollered, "Jonah! You get on home, you hear?" but the shoreside children had vanished. She sighed as the baby stirred again. "If that boy's still out, ma'am, I might have to ask you to hold the baby while I get the fire up."

A reversal so complete that Matt smiled at their backs as they walked up the hill together.

"If you would trust me, then I should be pleased to do so," Janiri answered. "This, too, I will need to know."

A soft whistle caught Matt's attention. "One of the neighbor girls said you were here, Cap'n. I wasn't sure if I should believe that." Will stood leaning against a pine tree, arms folded.

"I couldn't think where else to bring her, where she might be treated as a friend. She's lonely," Matt said. "I've been distracted."

"You been gutted is what you been."

Matt gave a soft huff of recognition. "I need to get up a lawsuit against Lee, though I know I'm on shaky ground without a contract on my side. Either way, it'll take money and time."

Will nodded. "What you got in that rucksack?"

Matt had almost forgotten the warm sack over his shoulder. "Half-burned woodcock. I wasn't joking when I said she needs cooking help."

Will chuckled. "Even if I won't come over for dinner, you bring it to me. You are a hard man to say no to, Matt Percy."

"Unless your name is Lee."

"Tell you what goes well with burnt meat: a shot of whiskey."

Matt looked at his friend. "You think?"

"Come on—I'm pouring."

CHAPTER THREE
March, 1867

SNOW SWIRLED IN THE AIR around the men gathered by the edge of Center Pond. When he left home, Janiri had been outside in the storm, delighting in the snowflakes that melted on her outstretched arms, as if she could embrace all of winter. Matt tucked his gloved hands under his arms, his woolen coat a strong defense against the wind. The crew would need a dozen men today, maybe a few more to clear the ice as the sawyers got to work, but at least four dozen stood in huddled groups or alone, shoulders hunched, hoping. Fishermen, lumbermen, farmers, all of them with no work, and nothing left in the larder by this bleak time of winter. "March Hill," they called it: the long slow trudge back to springtime, when the hunting grew scarce and families grew hungry. This time last year, Matt'd been on the other side of the crew, supervising the cutting and hauling of the load he carried over the sea. Today, he stood with the hopeful and despairing. The other men's stomachs would be knotted with hunger, their wives thin and drawn, their families sickly. Other men's wives couldn't make a meal of a single bone, nor keep the house warm without coal or firewood, at least when the pregnancy did not ail her. And as for the rest, her cooking improved under Susan's supervision, and she was careful to work no sorcery where others could see.

Last thing he wanted was for the townsfolk to grow even more suspicious than they already were. A man in his circumstances who didn't suffer by March had either mischief or witchcraft on his side, and Matt didn't want them suspecting the latter, or confirmed about the former. Janiri's sorcerous suppers grew thin with her time approaching. The pregnancy continued to be difficult at best, straining both her sorcery and herself, besides they needed the money to pay a lawyer against Lee's seizure of the gold, a case no sane man would accept just on the promise of winning. Matt stamped his feet, his breath coming in clouds around his face. Will had found work as a carpenter in the shipyard at Bath, offering to introduce Matt to the foreman, but he didn't want to be that far away from Janiri, not now. If the boss didn't hire him on today, he'd go home and read to her. His mother left behind a fair number of volumes from a subscription service out of Boston. These last two weeks, while Matt looked for work or hunted the sparse woodlands, the Darlings' oldest boy, Jonah, stayed at the house, ready in case Janiri should need help. He joined in the reading and played a lively fiddle to accompany Matt's rather shaky pianoforte. Sometimes, Janiri danced, her hips and shoulders swaying, and he wondered if she imagined herself back home, in whatever between-place her family truly occupied. And at the annual Christmas Ball, they'd danced together, flowing like the ocean.

"Percy! Matthew Percy, you want the job or not?"

Matt's head snapped up. "Sorry, yes. Where do you want me?"

The crew boss Roger Minott, a man he'd known all

his life, frowned at him, and Matt realized he'd been supporting his right shoulder again. "You up to this?"

"The war left me more than memories, but I can cut ice." Matt squared his shoulders. "Where do you want me?"

"Can you handle a horse?"

"Yes, sir."

Minott pointed toward a team hitching a huge Belgian draft horse to a large bar that dragged a set of blades to cut sections into the ice, an innovation that saved labor—or cost jobs, depending who you asked. Last year, Matt's crew used a horse-drawn saw, shaving days off their time. "You're with the Morse boys. You've got a lick of sense at least—see they don't do anything foolish."

Matt grinned. "Yes, sir."

Minott gave a nod and marked something in the sheaf of papers he carried. "Your wife's expecting?"

"Any day now."

"All best to her."

"Thank you, sir."

"Roger's fine." Roger Minott stared at him a long moment, then said, "Not everybody thinks Lee's in the right on this. You pulled off a bloody fine voyage. I'm sorry my father didn't agree to back you when you came to us."

"Not as sorry as I am, Roger."

Roger snorted, his breath curling mist into the air. "That's the truth, I warrant. Go on." Before Matt could thank him again, Roger moved past to the next man, pulling five more out of the crowd before he put away his papers and gave a sharp whistle.

Matt kicked through the snow toward the Morse brothers and the three other men of their team. One of them, Jed Tripp, Matt recognized from his crew and gave a nod. Tripp didn't acknowledge him, taking up a shovel and starting to clear the snow from the ice before them. Taking the horse's halter, Matt stroked its nose. "Bit cold, eh?" he murmured to the horse, letting it smell him and hear his voice.

"Right. So the boy clears snow, you lead the horse straight on where we tell you. I manage the gear and David works the reins," Samuel Morse explained. "These two walk either side to check our depth." The other two men, muffled in thick scarves and hats, took up their positions. They might have been Negro or white—they didn't reveal enough skin to know.

"Get on with it—I don't want to be out here all day," David said, and Samuel worked a lever to drop the blades. They crunched down into the ice, and, after a few more adjustments, Samuel stepped back and David flicked the reins. The horse gave a snort of mist and strained forward against its harness, tugging the ice cutter into motion. It carved down into the ice, making a resonant whine as the steel blades sank in. Matt walked slow beside the horse, keeping it straight on the path that Tripp was clearing, stopping when the Morses said so. The horse's heavy tread echoed in the ice as well, and Matt could sense the pattern of the movements, just as he could sense the quality of waves that struck the hull of his boat. Sawblades biting, hooves tramping, the lighter tread of the men alongside, and Tripp's lonely task of shoveling up ahead. They ought to take it in shifts to shovel like that, and he wondered if

Roger were open to that suggestion. He didn't know as his arm would do well with shoveling, but he'd give it a go if his turn came up.

All the long, weary morning, they worked their way across the pond, up and back, lifting the blades at the end of each row and re-positioning the horse and rig before carving the next one some distance away. Once they completed a pass, the rest of the crew came up to float and haul away the cut ice on sledges. Matt's nose felt numb and he longed for the comfort of his own parlor. Was Jonah reading to Janiri even now, or had she stepped outside into the snow, to let the crystalline beauty decorate her hands and hair and lashes. Tripp straightened from time to time and set a hand to his back, then got back to work.

As they approached the end of their run, where they'd have to lift the blades and turn the rig for the next pass, the steady ice beneath his feet tremored. Tripp paused, and Matt, too, hesitated, planting his feet. The thrum of movement through the ice remained different. The horse tossed its ears, snorting at him for stopping while the man behind flicked the reins.

"What's the trouble?" David called out, and Samuel rounded the gear to come up beside Matt.

"Why'd you stop?"

Matt looked ahead to Tripp, who put his head down. "The feel of the ice changed. There was a…a bounce, like a rogue wave. It still doesn't feel the same; I don't know if it'll support us, not this whole rig."

"It doesn't feel the same? Lord Christ." Samuel rolled his eyes. "Have you missed the storm beating down on us, Percy? You look like a snowman. It's plenty cold enough for good ice."

"I won't deny that, but there's a spring feeds into the pond not far from here. That's why it's deeper at this end. Any change in the flow can alter the ice."

"Do I look like a fool? I know that." Samuel set his jaw then stalked forward, examining the ice.

"Come on, let's go!" David shouted from behind the horse.

"We're checking the ice," Matt shouted back against the wind.

At Samuel's direction, Tripp scraped the fresh layer of snow off the ice and they peered down at it together. Samuel shrugged and started back toward him. "Looks fine to me."

It wasn't the look of the ice, but the feel that worried Matt.

"Good, let's get it done!" David hollered back. "Hya!" He smacked the reins and the horse lurched forward, Matt stumbling to catch up. Samuel jumped back out of the way. His foot slipped, and Tripp turned aside to steady him. Too late—Samuel's feet slid from under him and he crashed to the ground.

The ice cracked.

"Ho! Whoa there!" Matt shouted, hauling on the horse's lead, the nail-heads on his soles skidding.

"Get up," David called as he pulled on the reins. "Get out of there."

"No," shouted Matt and Tripp at the same time. The Negro threw himself flat, thrusting out the shovel as Matt dropped to his knees reaching toward them. "Stay low," said Matt.

Even as he said it, Samuel staggered to his feet and

the ice shifted beneath him. He had time for a scream before the broken ice pitched him backward into a splash of water. Samuel's flailing arms broke the surface, groping across the edge of the ice. Tripp scrambled toward the horse to no avail as the cracks spread and plunged him into the water.

The horse jerked its head, whinnying, unable to move backward with the blades grinding into the ice. Sweet Lord, in moments, they'd all be done for. "Get the gear up, David! Get that rig out of the way." Matt shouted. He flung himself flat on the ice. "Tripp! The shovel."

Tripp's head broke the surface, the shovel waving, then he gasped a breath and steadied long enough to push the shovel back in Matt's direction. Matt grabbed the handle and hauled backward, dragging Tripp up onto the stable ice. He kept pulling, shifting his grip until Tripp could grab his arm, and pull past him, crawling to safety, drenched and shaking.

"Samuel! Samuel, can you hear me?" Matt howled into the storm. The black mouth of water opened jaggedly before him, cracks creeping outward, then a hand waving, a face, frantic in profile, too far away to be reached with the shovel. Crowley's corpse overlaid the image in memory. By God, he would not lose another to the ice, but neither would he throw his own life away, not now. Shit. Behind him, David fumbled with the heavy gear, the reins forgotten, as one of the others helped Tripp back to shore. Matt got hold of the nearside rein, sliding the leather thong free of the brass loops that held it, then he slithered along the ice, his visibility shrinking to a few feet around him, but whether that was an effect of the snow or of his own racing mind, he could not tell.

There, Samuel's face, his hair sticking up and scattered with snow, his lips parted for a desperate breath. The leather rein wrapping his fist, Matt let himself slide into the water. It sucked him into its frigid grasp. He caught a deep breath and reached for Samuel, dragging the other man near even as he went under. Water closed over his head and he gagged on it. He shoved Samuel above him, struggling against the water's pull to keep them both afloat. His vision dimmed but his feet brushed the bottom and he thrust off, powering into Samuel's side, grappling with him as he kicked both of them toward the edge. He blinked at the swirling snow, trying to clear his vision. Kicking hard, he shoved Samuel up ahead of him. Samuel kicked just as hard, battering Matt's face and arms.

"Back!" He shouted, or tried to, through chattering teeth. "Pull back." His head cracked against the ice, a stinging blow instantly numb. Water rushed into his mouth and he choked on it.

The horse whinnied again, then the leather strap went taut and tore into Matt's arm. His shoulder wrenched hard and he screamed. Frigid water clung to him, dragging him down, his arm straining, but he remained sunk from the chest down, holding Samuel to his chest with his left arm so stiff he swore it had already frozen. Stupid, stupid, stupid, and now to be the death of them both. Two wishes. Was now the time, the moment of last resort when nothing could save him but her and her magic? Was this some new strain of Yankee tenacity, his refusal to wish—and would he die for it?

He coughed hard, his throat scoured as he coughed up water. "Back," he cried again.

The horse snorted, misting the air, backing away step by step and dragging them along the ice. Samuel was torn from him, and someone was shouting. The ice shivered beneath him—not safe yet. His body convulsed, and he couldn't stop coughing, his chest racked with pain.

Hands grabbed at him dragging him across the ice even as his soaked clothing threatened to freeze him fast to this dread prison. "Watch that arm!" Roger's voice. "Be careful."

"Got him, sir," David's voice.

Matt shook uncontrollably. He longed for the steady calm of Will Johnson. Oh, sweet Jesus, for the heat of Janiri's touch. "Janiri," he whispered through numbed lips. His hair stuck out in red icicles, tinkling as they struck together while the men bundled him off the pond. Other men's coats, warm from their bodies wrapped his shoulders and legs. He blacked out, sinking all over again.

"Where is my husband?" Janiri's voice, clear and strong, cut through the chatter of teeth and the babble of men.

"Get them to the hall, hurry! We need a fire."

"You shouldn't be here, ma'am."

"Where else should I be when Matthew needs me?" Then she was beside him, pressing between the hurrying men who carried him. They burst through the doors into—what—a tall building with a peaked roof. The church itself. They lay him on the floor, and her hands stroked over his face. He blinked, the ice melting away at her touch, her warmth enveloping him as she embraced him, cradling his face against her throat.

"The fire," he whispered. "For all of us."

Her kiss shot heat through his forehead. For a moment, she was gone and his trembling returned. A crackle, then a roar, and someone whooped. "God, but that woman can strike a match." A hiccup of startled laughter. "Sorry, Pastor."

She returned, bundling Matt against her, the mound of her pregnant belly between them. Her heat seeped into him, easing the strain at his chest and fighting back the dead weight that clutched his legs.

"We should strip their wet clothes, sir," someone pointed out.

"Not with a woman present," another man protested.

"You can hardly have any doubt I have seen a naked man before." Her hot fingers worked through the tangles of his hair, then she peeled away the frozen gloves that encased his numb fingers. Any part of him not too cold to feel throbbed with pain. Pain streaked from his shoulder, worse than it had ever been before. "I shall be so angry, Matthew Percy, if you never again dance with me." Her words a hot breeze across his ear.

"Not so angry as I'll be with myself," he whispered, shaking in her embrace. All the things he could have lost in a moment's impulse. What was a ship or a chest of gold, compared with this, with life itself and all the bounty it had to offer?

Her belly clenched between them, a sudden squeeze, and he felt her throat pulse with a stifled cry. "It's coming?" he asked, his throat feeling rough, his lips cracked with cold.

"Soon. Do not worry."

He relaxed into her arms, his breath still coming short, his lungs burning. He closed his eyes and sank back into the darkness.

***

Matt woke with a jolt to the sound of her screaming. He bolted upright on a cushioned bench and nearly fell, his right arm bound tight against his chest. "Janiri!" The gloom of the raging storm closed in the windows of the church, but the glow of the stove still warmed the corner where he lay. A pile of wet clothing steamed gently by the stove.

"That you, Cap'n?' One of the others rolled over, blinking at him. "Surprised to see you up." Tripp's dark face peered from a swaddle of blankets.

"Tripp, where's my wife?" Matt glanced around, spotting Samuel similarly wrapped in blankets, snoring softly on the floor by the stove. He pushed up with his left arm, swinging his legs down to the floor, bare feet meeting the wood. Beside his long, pale foot lay a patch of dark-stained wood edged with soot. Blood and fire.

"They're taking care of her, Cap'n. You got to rest now."

Another scream, muffled by the walls between them. "No, I don't. Where is she?"

A man hurried over from the other corner, clapping his hands together. "Ah, Mr. Percy, so glad to see you improving, but I do think you should rest."

"I think I should be with my wife, Pastor."

"Vestry," mumbled Samuel, his eyes fluttering open. "Roger got in the doctor for you both. She didn't want to wake you."

Was he truly expected to sleep through her terrible screams? Matt lurched to his feet, shedding a few blankets and, swaying, searching for the door. Samuel unburied a hand and pointed. "Thanks, Matt," he said hoarsely. "I'll take you on my crew any time."

"Mr. Percy, truly, Doctor Greene is with her, and I don't know that—"

Making no reply, Matt stumbled across the floor, using the backs of the benches for balance. His shoulder throbbed with pain, but the doctor's binding kept it from moving. The chill beyond the stove struck him immediately, stinging his freshly warmed skin. Blood spattered the floor in places along the aisle, and in other places, dark scorch marks as if from dropped coals. As if she were falling apart. As if the child she carried tore her to pieces from within. They had spoken of her pregnancy—would the baby come in water or in flame? Could Janiri even hold her human form through the birthing? What if she died and he lost them both? No, no, no. Matt reached the door and flung it open, more strongly than he intended. His muscles still twitched with the icy bath he'd taken. Without her, he would be dead now, his heart frozen as surely as Crowley's had been. In the cramped vestry, Janiri lay on a pile of cushions and drapery, her knees up. Doctor Greene knelt by her feet, his sleeves rolled back and blood streaking his hands and arms. The pastor's wife, Mrs. Drury, sat at Janiri's head, stroking her hair as she sobbed red-shimmering tears.

The other two glanced at him, their faces drawn and worried, both beaded with sweat. How hard Janiri must be holding back not to burst into flame right now.

"She's got a powerful fever," Mrs. Drury said. "P'raps its good you've come."

"She always runs warm," Matt replied as he sank down by his wife. "Janiri, can you hear me?"

Janiri whimpered, giving a tiny nod, her hand waving toward him, and he caught it in his left, gripping hard. With every contraction of her body, her hand pulsed hot against his own.

"Coming all this way like she did, in that kind of weather, it's probably strained her too much," the doctor muttered. "Has the pregnancy been difficult?"

"Very." He leaned in close, her heat giving him strength. "You can do this, Janiri. You're so strong."

"If I had been called in sooner, I might have been able to provide more support. The child's crested, but—"the doctor's cool gaze assessed Janiri's hips and thighs. "Well. What's needed is a bit more pushing, I'd say."

Janiri's teeth clenched, and fire singed Matt's hand but he did not let go. Mrs. Drury cried out along with Janiri as her belly heaved. "The fever, Doctor, it's getting worse!"

He wished they would both shut up and leave him alone, leave her alone. They could not help her, not while she warred with her own nature to bring forth a child of them both. His heart stuttered, as it had in that frigid pool when he felt certain he must die. When he thought to wish for his own deliverance. Had she even the strength now to grant it? Her body convulsed, and he bit down on a curse as pain flared between his fingers. The thin gold band of her wedding ring, his mother's ring, melted and dripped to the floor, searing along his fingers He tore his hand away, gasping and plunged it into the basin of water that awaited his child's birth. The gold shimmered in a large drop on the floor reflecting his pale face. Janiri's eyes widened, staring up at him, damp with apology, then they slid shut; she whimpered, a sound he'd never heard from her before, a sound that shocked him more than the icy water.

Doctor Greene bent over Janiri's belly with a stethoscope stuck in his ears. His lips crumpled, and Matt hardly needed his next words. "The baby's heart rate is slowing," he muttered, as if he didn't want them to hear. They were losing the baby, and blood streaked Janiri's thighs.

Glaring at the pastor's wife sent the woman a few inches back, her eyes wide and blinking as if astonished by the fever in his own. Matt leaned in close and stroked back Janiri's wild hair, waves of heat rising to his touch. "Janiri—" he waited through a pulse of pain and fire—"I wish our child were born with no further trouble. Can you do that? Can you do it now? I wish—"

"I heard you!" she screamed, then gave a moan.

"Push, that's a good girl," the doctor called, but Janiri cried again and gripped Matt's hand, the tender burns flaring with pain.

Matt closed his eyes, resting his forehead against hers as she sobbed. One more cry, a shriek of unearthly pain and fear, bound with words that singed his face to hear them. A rush passed through him, as if he were the ocean and her voice were the wave. It left him faintly dizzy, adrift for a moment in a place that swirled with stars and streaked with fire.

"Yes, yes," the doctor exulted. "Mary, do you have a

blanket. Where's that basin?"

"Here, Doctor." Mrs. Drury shifted, her departure leaving a cooler void near Matt's head.

"Is it done?" he whispered.

"You," Janiri panted. "You wish for the smallest things."

"Keep pushing. A little more," the doctor urged, then, "yes!"

Fleshy damp sounds, followed by a cry, startled and young. "It's a girl," the doctor announced. "My, she is a big one, and so pink!"

A few tears slid down Matt's cheeks, and he lifted his head, gazing into Janiri's eyes. "What is life but little things?"

The baby's crying slowed, and Matt sat up, a spark of fear returning, but he could see the child nestled in Mrs. Drury's arms while the doctor examined it. She rocked the baby gently, crooning to it, but its gaze roved as if it could take in every detail of the small chamber and the world that greeted it. For a long moment, the doctor remained at Janiri's feet, pressing down on her abdomen, then examining her more closely. He nodded to himself, then edged around, coming to squat by Janiri's head. He pressed a hand to her damp forehead and listened to her heart. "The fever seems to have broken as well, Mr. Percy. But she's lost a fair amount of blood. We'll need to keep a close watch the next day or so." He slung his stethoscope over his neck. "I understand you've been in rather straitened circumstances, Matthew, but you should know you can come to me if you or your family are sick. We'll make an arrangement."

"Thank you, Doctor."

"Are you ready to hold her, Mrs. Percy?" Mrs. Drury asked.

"I do not know," said Janiri, but she managed a smile. Her silky hair lay plastered to her face and tangled all around her, her favorite ruffled gown damp and stained. She slipped her hand away and reached for their baby.

"That shoulder, Mr. Percy. It's not a simple dislocation as I expect you know. That's happened before."

Matt nodded, not taking his eyes from the tiny child curled into his wife's arms. Wrinkled and pink, with little curls of dark hair across her scalp, miniature hands and feet pulled close to her body.

"Mr. Percy." Matt looked up at the new tone in the doctor's voice. "You've torn it rather badly, internally, I mean. Aside from the damage to your muscles and tendons, I suspect nerve damage as well. We shall need to check for that when the inflammation has died down. In any event, it'll likely be months before you can work, and you may never regain full movement."

Matt blinked at him, the words taking a little while to penetrate. Months before he could work. Never regain full movement. With every gift he received, something of himself was stripped away. "Then I'll learn to tie a bowline left-handed."

The doctor shook his head, but started packing up his kit while Mrs. Drury fussed over the makeshift bedding they had gathered. "I'll come out and check on you all in a few days. You'll both need a good deal of rest. Aside from the arm, you've nearly drowned, and in freezing water. There'll be consequences—infection of the lungs is a strong possibility. Do you understand me? I presume, Mary, that they may stay here at least the night, and likely tomorrow? They both need rest."

"Oh, certainly, Doctor. We'd not turn out a babe so new in any case. I expect today's miracles may provide Mr. Drury with a sermon on Sunday."

"I'd best check on the others." Doctor Greene nodded to them both, then let himself out.

Janiri shifted around at Matt's side, opening her bodice and tucking the baby close in to her breast. She murmured to it in her own language, the one she so rarely used. Matt lay down on his left side, watching them, letting Mrs. Drury tuck him in with a thick woolen blanket, his head pillowed on his good arm. Almost his only arm. He dispelled the thought by studying his daughter's face, her little body clutched so close to her mother's breast, both of them now draped with a blanket of their own. "I'll just go warm some cider, shall I?'" Then Mrs. Drury retreated from the little chamber and shut the door.

His shivering returned, but not so badly now. "Clara," he rasped. "Let's call her Clara."

"Why that name?" Janiri took her eyes from the baby to look over at him. Her eyes were shadowed, her face drawn. How close had he come to losing her?

"It's the name of a battlefield nurse, from the war." His throat ached, his lungs flaring with pain at each breath. "Angel of the Battlefield, we called her."

Janiri's tired eyes warmed, a glow of fire returning. "Will she be an angel?"

"Not with you and I for parents. Will she be like you?"

"A little like me, a little like you." Her lips hinted at a smile, then she said, "Go to sleep, Matthew, and I will be here."

The emotions that had washed through his body from the despair of the frigid water to the fear of losing her to the joy of gazing into Clara's eyes finally ebbed away again, leaving him drained and peaceful. Sleep began to sound like a fine idea. And she would be there. "How did you know I needed you?"

"Ah, Matthew," she breathed. "I will always hear you call my name." She broke eye contact and gathered baby Clara upon her chest, the baby's soft head resting just below her chin. Very softly, she began to hum, a lilting melody that reminded him of the circle dancing on the night of their wedding. He closed his eyes and let the rhythm take him, drifting and spiraling out among the stars, like the sudden opening of his heart as he made his wish.

***

Matt slept on and off for days—mostly on, truth be told. The doctor's boy delivered a brown vial of medicine for the pain, but it made his mind soft and churned his stomach. Most of those days, Janiri lay beside him, with Clara in a cradle at her side, and Jonah Darling coming and going from the bedside, bringing soups that Matt couldn't remember anyone making. Was her sorcery growing easier now that the baby had been born? God—what if Jonah had noticed?

That roused Matt enough to look around. Janiri's place lay empty, the cradle empty at its side. The curtains spread from the window to show a broad horizon of blue-gray over the dense pine forest. Storm coming, or storm receding? Hard to tell. He worked himself to the side of the bed, clinging to the post with his left hand as he swung his feet down. His right still lay bound against his chest, immobilizing his shoulder so it could heal, to the extent that it ever would. A length of rope coiled on the floor where he'd thrown it after trying to tie even an overhand knot with his left hand. He hadn't expected to be so crippled. The fingers of his right hand moved weakly at his command. They would strengthen—they had to. He found a shirt draped over the foot of the bed and shrugged it over his good arm, pulling the other shoulder up over the sling. Each button required separate concentration, but he managed it after a while. That done, and after using the chamber pot—how much did he owe Susan's son for emptying that thing while he lay in bed half-dazed—he hunted up the rest of his clothes. His chest still ached a little with every breath, though Doctor Greene had said the sensation would fade. Wasn't the first time he was fished from the water—God willing, it wouldn't be the last or he was no sailor.

Trousers hung on a peg by the door, and that took a bit of work, getting his feet in, not losing his balance. Thank God for braces, pulled up one by one and hitched over his shoulders. Socks proved to be utterly impossible. No matter, the chill of the floor kept him alert. He reached for his lucky cap, the one that saw him through the war, through the adventure of Janiri's isle. His hand hung in the air over the empty peg. Damn—where had it gone, and when? Flown from his head in the gale out on Center Pond? Or plunged into the water beneath the ice? Come springtime, when the world thawed out again, it might be found, sodden and more worn than ever, lucky once more. Or maybe that, like the rest of his luck, was gone forever. He closed his fist, empty.

The mirror over the dresser showed his face lean and haggard, his mustache and beard grown scruffy without any tending. Come springtime, when the weather grew warm, that, too, could go. If he could work out how to shave left-handed without carving off his own nose. His nose had always been a bit sharp and long in any case. His eyes looked more mossy than emerald today, his hair sticking up in clumps. He found a comb and awkwardly encouraged his hair to lie flat again. It swept lower than his brows and curled over his ears, down past his collar at the back, the way she liked it. He would have tugged his hair into a queue and tied it off with a bit of ribbon, but that again was a thing he could not manage one-handed.

His coat hung on a peg of its own. Matt eyed it, then ignored it as he pulled open the door and made his slow way down the stairs. They set a little crooked, to emulate the tilt of a ship's deck, his father claimed—or simply because his grandfather'd been drunk when he laid them, as Matt thought more likely. Through the left-hand door into the parlor, Matt saw Janiri, sound asleep, her head tipped to the side, over the baby's. She occupied his grandmother's rocker, baby to her breast and a shawl spread over both of them. To the right, from the kitchen, came the soft sounds of someone working, then, still softly as if not to disturb the mother and child, the sound of someone whistling. Matt ducked through the doorway. "Will?"

Will looked up from the basin of water, a towel over his shoulder, and put down the pot he was scrubbing. In three strides he caught Matt in his embrace, crushing him to his chest. "Sweet Lord, Matt, don't you do that again, you hear me? You don't go under less'n I'm there to pull you back out."

"My God, Will, I wish you had been." Matt wrapped his friend with his left arm, and took in a deep breath, taking in his simple human warmth and the smell of sawdust and herbs. He hadn't realized until that moment how much he missed him. "Maybe I wouldn't be so broken if you had."

"Can't trust a horse to handle a man gentle, that's the truth." After a moment, Will drew back and studied him critically. "What's the doc say?"

"Nerve damage." Matt glanced around the kitchen, taking in the stack of unfamiliar crockery and the bins of last year's potatoes and carrots stacked by the door.

"So, what's that mean? Is it coming back or no?" Splashing began behind him as Will got back to work on the dishes.

Another long breath, shaky this time, his lungs still aching. "Hard to say. It'll take a while. Have to let the muscle recover before I try to use it."

"Could be done for?" Will asked softly.

Matt closed his eyes, letting the kitchen's familiarity wash over him. The wide pine floors, smooth with age, comforted his bare feet in spite of the chill at floor level. Could he steer a ship one-handed? Hold his baby? Dance with his wife? His eyes burned and he squeezed the bridge of his nose until the sensation retreated. "Aye, it could be."

Dishes clinked, water sloshed, a towel squeaked over something. "You got a plan yet? I know you're always working on a plan."

"Not yet." He crossed to the sink in the corner where the iron hand pump stood, its handle waiting for a few strong pulls. Shit.

"You want me to—"

"No." Matt reached out with his left hand, depositing a pitcher from the windowsill into the sink. He shifted how he stood to grab the handle and pump. It took a few tries before the water pulled through the cold pipes, then he got a full pitcher. It was awkward, but possible. He retrieved a mug from the hooks overhead and set it down, pouring carefully. Every task took too much concentration, and he could feel Will's eyes on him before the sounds of dish-washing resumed. Matt took a long drink of ice-cold water. It cooled his throat, and he felt a little taller, a little stronger when he set the mug back down. "Admiral Nelson fought the battle of Trafalgar with only one arm, y'know."

"Ain't he the one they brought home in a whiskey barrel?"

Matt steadied himself with another long swallow, then turned to face his friend, leaning against the edge of the soapstone sink. "Is that why you're in my kitchen washing somebody else's dishes?"

"I came when I heard what happened, but I got to get back in two days, or the job's not waiting. Now I've seen you, I'll tell 'em I need to stay."

"No, you won't. You've got a chance, Will, you keep hold of it. There's no point both of us drowning in the undertow."

Will's jaw worked. "Don't you tell me you don't need me. Jonah's just a boy, Mother's helper, sure, but this is way beyond your wife learning to cook, Matt. What're you going to do? You got a family, now."

"I don't know!" The words came out hard as gunshots, and Matt hung his head, propping his forehead in his hand. "I don't know. I don't know what kind of a life I can give them, like this. It's bad enough I've got no ship and nothing to show for the voyage, now there's this."

Whatever he was doing, Will put it down, and the floor creaked as he walked over. "After the war I didn't know where to go or what to do. Come home with me, you said, there's always work for willing hands."

Willing hands. Two of them. Still, it had taken a few months before Will appeared on his doorstep. "I remember," Matt said, his voice strangled.

"You had this notion, let's sail to Africa and sell ice, and we did that. Don't matter that we got nothing from it but your wife. You said, let's do it. You made that happen. What, five, six shipyards turned you down? Didn't stop you from asking again."

"Matt?" Janiri called from the parlor. "Is that you?"

"Yes—I'll be there. Give me a minute."

"Alright," she said, a word that rolled on her tongue. She knew how it made him feel, but today, he could not muster a smile.

"I was counting on the lawsuit, but I can't afford a lawyer if I can't work." Matt lifted his head. Sturdy half-timbers spanned the ceiling and clean plaster covered the walls between the fine glass windows. "Might be I could sell the house. That'd give us a bit of cash to start with. I know there's some would like to have the land, and the view of the bay."

Will leaned against the sink beside him, their shoulders brushing. "Your family built this house, that right?"

He nodded wearily. "Janiri doesn't even like Phippsburg, maybe there's another place to go where it's not so hard."

"I can't imagine you any place but here, Matt."

Neither could he, and that, right there, was the trouble. Sailing in the summertime, or lumbering or fishing. Ice cutting in the wintertime. And him already on the outs with half the town thinking him a thief or a pirate—a murderer, even—looking down on him for his choice of friends or his choice of bride. Maybe it was time to up and go and leave behind everything he'd ever known, almost everything he'd ever loved or dreamed or wanted. But that's why he'd been in bed these last few days, looking for a way to accept that his dreams had gone. Unless he wished again. Was it worth a wish, this time, to save his livelihood and his home? His last wish? And what happened when things got truly dire, when no effort of his could save a life—when Clara took a fall while riding, or Janiri's fire grew out of control, or some damned lynch gang showed for Will for getting too uppity? He still had choices. Save the wish for the moment his choices ran out. "I always thought I'd be buried here," he whispered.

"There's got to be another way. I mean, we don't know your arm's ruined, do we? Folks from Parker's Head been bringing meals over. The pastor arranged it for you and your family. They'll keep you through the winter, anyhow. You'll find a way to hold out a few months, hold out 'til the summer, maybe longer, and then we'll see, right?"

Matt gave a breath of laughter. "I thought I was the dreamer, not you."

"You sound like you're digging your own grave and like to lay down in it."

"If I have to sell the house, it's got to happen by storm season, the end of summer, or we'll be stuck another winter."

A rap sounded on the front door, and both men straightened. "Come in," Janiri called from the parlor, before Matt decided if he even wanted visitors. The door creaked open and someone stepped into the hall, accompanied by a gust of cold wind and the sound of boots being scraped by the door.

"Thank you, ma'am," a man's voice replied.

Will's dark eyes met his. "We climbed out of that ditch together, Matthew Percy. Promise me you ain't gonna lie down easy."

"I'll do my best." Matt swallowed around the lump in his throat. "Better go see who that is." Might be easier at this point than staying in here, his chest aching, thinking about how to give up his life forever. Matt pushed through the hall into the parlor on the other side, avoiding the melting bits of snow that tracked where the visitor walked, thinking of the glassy steps of Janiri's people in the sand around a dead man. Matt wasn't dead, not yet, he just needed to think more about the things that made life worth living.

Janiri smiled up at him from the rocking chair. She

wore her hair in a single dark braid over the opposite shoulder, and it swayed with her rocking like a serpent prepared to hypnotize. A fire crackled at the hearth, where the visitor stood warming his hands. "Matthew. I'm right glad to see you up." Her companion, Samuel Morse, tucked his hat under his arm and stuck out his right hand, then he took in Matt's empty sleeve. His expression dimmed. He curled back his fingers and let his hand drop to his side.

"Glad to see you, too, Samuel. Looks like you've made a good recovery." Matt crossed to Janiri, who turned her face up for a kiss. He ran his fingers lightly down her cheek.

"Oh, aye. Better than you, it seems, but I didn't have somebody kicking on top of me, shoving me down." Samuel stood a few inches shorter than Matt, but broad in the chest, with a thick brown beard and a shipwright's hands. "That was me, wasn't it?" He nodded toward Matt's arm. "You got Tripp out alright, but I panicked so hard, I made everything worse on you."

"You could stand to lose a few pounds," Matt replied.

Samuel blinked at him, then laughed. "Thanks, Matt. I truly do not know how to express my gratitude. I'd be dead if you hadn't been there, and I know it."

"One of the others—"

He shook his head. "No, Matt, they wouldn't. They might've tried; they might've wanted to—but you saw it. Dropping the gear, grabbing the reins, getting the horse to haul us up. Like you had it all laid out in your head."

"I wish—" Matt began, then started over. "Had I thought a bit harder, maybe I'd've come up with something that didn't do so much damage."

"Had you thought a bit longer, I'd be a dead man." Samuel regarded him seriously. "I came over about your bill with Doctor Greene."

Matt stiffened. He hadn't even thought of that—his own treatment, plus Janiri's. Even without the usual expenses, that would devour what little savings remained.

Shaking his head, Samuel continued, "That's not what I meant, Matt—not at all. I wanted to tell you, it's covered. Medicine, surgery, anything you need. Greene's to send me the bill. For your family, too."

The gloom that bore him down lifted just a little. "Thanks, Samuel. That means a lot."

"It is a great kindness," Janiri echoed, her voice rich, and he saw a hint of a flush in Samuel's cheeks as he avoided looking at her.

"Nobody should climb March Hill alone, not after what you've done. Speaking of, Roger Minott sent this over." He searched through a few pockets, and came up with a card, offering it to Matt who pinched it between his fingers.

The card bore an unfamiliar name, Joseph Banks, followed by an address in Bath and the single word, "solicitor."

"Roger's brother-in-law. When you're ready to take on Old Man Lee, you're to call on him."

A card worth its weight—and more—in gold. Matt grinned. "Now that is some thanks." He slipped the card into his sling for safe-keeping. "We've been waiting on word from Tenerife, to see if the pilot and the shore crew will support my word. Ever since the storms began, I worry that ship's not ever coming home."

"I believe it will," said Janiri softly. "But I cannot say when."

Samuel's thick brows pinched together. "Didn't know what to think—begging your pardon, ma'am—of a sale for gold with no contract to speak of. Seemed a mite worrisome, like the old man said. That's not how things're done. But you got a raw deal out of him, and that's a fact. The tide's turned around town. You've always been a bit fey, Matt, if you don't mind my saying, and the plan to take a crew of Negroes out to sell ice to more of them sounded mad." Samuel fiddled with the hat in his hands. "Opinion wasn't hard in your favor. Then when you returned, we started hearing rumors round the shipyards, how you and your man were criminals, how you drugged your crew to pull the switch and bring in the gold, that Crowley'd got wind of the truth. Sounded like a bad business." Samuel shrugged awkwardly. "Like I say, the tide's turned. Would a thief be out on the ice in a gale like that? No, sir, he'd be thinking up a way to steal what he wanted—to get it the easy way. Would a murderer risk himself to save another? What you did—it got us thinking, a lot of us."

Matt studied him thoughtfully, the man he might have sacrificed his future to save. "That's not why I did it."

"I know it. That's what makes it true." Samuel pushed his hat onto his head. "Congratulations on your new family, Matt. I won't keep you." He walked toward the door, retrieving a cloak from its peg by the fire, and Matt walked with him, to see him to the door.

"Come to think of it, Matt." Samuel swung the cloak

up onto his shoulders and squared himself while he fastened the clasp. "When you get your gold, you come to us. We'll build you a finer ship than that *Diana*, for sure. You don't want any piece of Old Man Lee. The Morse yard'll be happy to get your trade."

"But you're in steamships now."

"Steam is the future, Matt. Think it over." He tipped his hat. "Good day, Ma'am."

Matt shut the door behind him and turned back to his wife. The ache in his arm, the burning in his chest, they were as nothing to this new sensation spreading from the card tucked in his sling.

"Do you know, people have been bringing us food, and baby things as well?" Janiri indicated a pot that hung over the fire. "People I do not even know. I thought perhaps that Susan came to cook, but it is not she."

"She and the others on Malaga are working too hard to climb March Hill themselves." He walked back and sank gratefully onto a bench at her side. "Our family used to send things over there, this time of year. Extra clothes, blankets, food."

"And now you are repaid." She frowned. "But not by them."

"It's called charity. It's what we do for each other, to keep each other going."

"Even if there is no payment, nor even friendship."

"Don't your people take care of each other?"

"Our lives are not so fragile, and there is always the spark. If we need food, we have it. If we need to get away, we are gone. If we need help, we conjure it." She cocked her head, her eyes distant and mysterious. "When my people gather, we speak of yours, of the meetings and agreements, the bargains. The wishes. Men wish for women. They wish for gold and for power. These things all, they wish for, so the stories tell. And so often it ruins them, these wishes of greed. Wishes of the earth."

"I'm not so different: I wished for you."

"You needn't have," she said shortly. "You are not so different, you say. At any moment, you may wish for Old Man Lee's head to be your punch bowl. You may wish for every ship in his yard or every coin of gold my father gave you—or more gold, even, than that. I keep waiting, listening, but you wish for none of these. You barely allow me to use my spark in service to you or to our home. Now these people, they bring us charity because you nearly died. You needn't have, Matthew, you might have wished to live."

For a moment, he remembered the water, the terrible burning in his lungs, the weight of his legs dragging him downward and the stiffening cold that gripped his hands and stopped up his throat. "I did. I wanted to live more than anything," he said, "but I did it by fighting, by trying harder and working more. I didn't need sorcery to make that wish come true." He ran his hand over his hair. "I even lost my lucky cap."

"You nearly died." Her words accused him, and he drew back, wary as the room grew hot.

Slowly, he nodded. "So did you," he answered, "and Clara with you. I believed that I could save myself. Just as I knew I couldn't save either of you. That's not a little thing, Janiri, when your life is as fragile as ours, it's the only thing. It's why they bring us food, and why, if I knew one of them couldn't work, even Old Man Lee himself, Janiri, I would do the same for them. Look at the snow piled up out there, and here it is nearly spring. Until now, it's been the work of my hands that keeps me warm, and so it is with everyone in Phippsburg. And if my hand can't do that anymore, there's another hand ready to help."

"You would bring soup to your enemy to feed him through the winter?"

"Sure. I'd stew it with poison ivy. It'd make his lips swell up something awful, but he wouldn't starve." He flashed her a grin. "Here, now, what should we read?" He walked over to the shelf of books.

Someone tapped at the parlor door, then Will entered, carrying a tray. "Tea's ready.

"Thank you, William." Janiri's smile broadened, and the baby shifted in her arms. "Sit with us, would you? Matthew will read me something." To Matt, she said, "*Uncle Tom's Cabin.*"

"Not on my account," Will said.

Matt reached for the book. "It's her favorite—we must've read it five times already this month."

"I like when the ice saves her life, she and her child both," Janiri explained. "The idea of a frozen river. Until I came here, I could not imagine it." She stroked the hair of the child in her arms, and probably didn't notice the ice that seemed to pass across Will's face. "Is it true that your people have suffered all of these things?" She looked up at Will, her face full of that innocent curiosity Matt ordinarily found so appealing.

The slender book hung in Matt's hand, a book that meant something completely different to his friend, and he said, "We can read something else, Will. It's fine. How about *Moby Dick?*"

"Anything but this! I cannot bear it," Janiri protested, but Will was already backing out the door.

"You go on. The snow's let up and I'd like to head over to Malaga for a spell if the crossing's good. You got each other now." Will nodded to himself as if they had readily agreed, then the door shut behind him. A few minutes later, the front door opened and shut as well.

Matt sank back onto his bench. "Janiri…"

"Why does he do this? I ask a question and he cannot give me any answer. Am I so offensive as this?"

"This one's not you. I'm not sure anyone can really know about slavery but someone who's lived through it."

"And your William has, hasn't he?"

He pressed the book beneath his palm and considered how much to tell her. "Will escaped. Four, five years ago. I don't know his story—he hasn't seen fit to share that, even with me. You've seen how folks around here treat the Negroes. Before the war, some were abolitionists like my family, but most never were. Half the sea-faring families hereabouts depended on shipping slave-grown Southern cotton, so they had plenty of incentive to support the rebels, openly or otherwise. It's so much worse for the escaped slaves, worse even than for the free-born Negroes. Folks make as if it's their own fault they were slaves, as if they're less than anybody else. Even in the 54th, all our men had to swear an oath they were never slaves before they could get their pay—and that was after all of us taking no pay for a year and a half because they weren't planning to pay the blacks as much as the whites. The major who wrote the oath phrased it carefully so they weren't exactly lying when they swore. As for Will—" he met her eyes and adopted some of her own ferocity. "I am the only man in town that knows the truth and I only know it because he gave up his shirt to staunch my bleeding."

He remembered that day all too well, crawling from the press of the dead, the cannons still firing overhead, his body slick with blood and he couldn't be sure how much was his own, but he wasn't feeling it yet. He scanned the sand around him from Colonel Shaw's body, face down on the ridge above him, to the waves of black men fallen in between. For a moment, Matt thought he might be the only survivor, then he heard a shout. Will lay trapped where a section of the fort's fencing came down on him, screaming for help. Down the beach, the horns blew a retreat, and any wounded who could still move fled toward the safety of the Union line. In moments, the rebels would swarm down the barricade into the ditch and slaughter any man who lived. Matt ran to his man and hauled on that fence for all he was worth. He managed it—barely—and Will scrambled out from under. A rifle shot slammed into Matt's side, twisting him round, his hand still clenched between the logs, and he felt the yank of his shoulder giving way as he collapsed. The rebs cheered, then roared their fury as Will got him up again and the two of them took off running. Beyond the next dune, under the fire of the Union guns, Will, a private Matt barely knew, stripped off his shirt, revealing the scars that streaked his back. Even then, Matt could see it cost him to reveal the truth.

To Janiri, he said, "Everybody else believes he was a

free man when he signed on with the army, and I am not ever letting them know any different. You can't let this slip."

"Thank you for trusting me." Her glance fell to the book in his lap as she shifted baby Clara to her shoulder, patting her back until she let out a burble. "Yes, I can imagine he would not wish to hear this story, not if he has lived it."

Matt felt sure there was more—that secret Will referred to, but he acknowledged he might never learn it. "*Moby Dick*, then?" he asked lightly.

"No. I wish even more to hear it now. When I was a child, learning about your world, I could only think that men made of dirt must be soft and weak, prepared to crumble at the slightest touch of fire. Now, I think there is strength to this earth that I cannot ever know."

"The author started writing the book while she was here in Maine, you know."

"Enough with your pride. Just read."

Matt opened the book on his lap, pinning it with his hand. "Chapter one," he read aloud, "In which the reader is introduced to a man of humanity..."

CHAPTER FOUR

September 1867

A FINE EARLY AUTUMN DAY warmed the tall windows of the courthouse and made Matt a little drowsy in spite of the tension that knotted his shoulders. The right one still ached despite the six months since his plunge through the ice. As they waited on the leather seats, Matt forced his hand to grip a bit of rope, turning the circle with his left, bringing through the end with his right, steadily, as if he were threading the eye of a needle instead of a hole broad enough for his fist. Bowline. One of the most basic knots of the sailor's craft. Before he finished the knot, his hand shook and the ache spread from his numb fingertips to his elbow. He could feel himself sweating, though Janiri had not been allowed in the courtroom apart from giving her testimony. She sat in the gallery above, and he heard Clara fussing from too much stillness. He couldn't blame her—he felt like fussing as well. They'd delayed the case all summer, hoping for word from Tenerife, to see if Tahari had been convinced to guide another ship to the island he feared so much. Lee's natural history voyage had not yet returned, though a trader from the area reported seeing it under sail pressing south along the African coast a few months earlier.

At Matt's side the solicitor, Joseph Banks, read through papers for another case. The notes for his own case occupied a very slim folder indeed, and September had already begun. The small crowd muttered in the ranks behind him, and, at the other side of the room, Charles Lee sat stiff as a mast flanked by three lawyers from Portland. Over the course of the half-hour since the judge went to his chamber, the four men of the opposition gradually all assumed the same position, their hands folded together on the table in front of them. They barely spoke now that arguments were done, in spite of the warm courtroom and the dragging minutes. Djinn were made of fire and men of earth, but maybe these ones were made of stone. Certainly Lee's heart had been. Matt worked the knot free and painstakingly started over.

"All rise!" the bailiff called.

"Now we've come to it," Joseph muttered.

"That was quick, wasn't it? You thought it might take hours."

Joseph shrugged. "Hard to say if that's a good sign." They shared a look as Matt dropped his length of rope and pushed back his chair, standing tall at Joseph's side. At the solicitor's suggestion, he had borrowed Will's Union cap for the occasion, and it rested on the table in front of him, reminding everyone of his status as a veteran of combat. Would it help? God only knew. He'd lay odds the judge had been a Southern sympathizer.

Wearing a stiff black robe, gavel in hand, Judge Cooper shuffled up the steps to take his seat behind a little wall, like a sniper behind his palisade.

At their table, Lee's staff stood as well.

"Be seated, gentlemen." The judge's glance flicked up to where Janiri sat in the gallery, the only woman present. He took his seat and, with a creaking of leather and scraping of wood, the litigants sat as well. Judge Cooper scanned the room, settling first on Lee, then on Matt, his eyes deep and watery as the Kennebec itself. "After reviewing the merits of the case, primarily the documentation provided by the defendant, as well as the testimony of those witnesses for the plaintiff"—those witnesses who were allowed to testify, the Negro majority of Matt's crew were not— "I have decided in favor of the defendant. The terms of the contract are clear, and without supporting evidence of this island and its occupants, we are forced to conclude that the plaintiff failed to fulfill its terms."

As he spoke the tide of Matt's fury rose. "But Your Honor! Twelve men swore they'd been to that island, and met the inhabitants. For God's sake, I married one of them!"

"These men." Judge Cooper pursed his lips. "They are widely acknowledged by Mr. Lee and by yourself to have been selected for their willingness rather than their fitness. Under such circumstances, and given that they were paid in gold prior to the receipt of and recording of the gold by your erstwhile employer, Mr. Lee, their testimony may be expected to be biased in your favor. This alleged uncharted island cannot be attested to by any source outside of that crew, Mr. Percy." He patted his forehead, and his glance flicked upward again. "As for your wife, a woman's bias in support of her own husband is one of the basic tenets of law, and even she admits she was not present during the negotiations nor the transfer of goods.

"That being said, this contract is the most clearly

one-sided document I have ever seen. If proof can be found of proper delivery, the Lee shipyard clearly owes you fair recompense, plus damages to your reputation and to your person during the period of escrow of the funds you would be owed. However, I repeat, unless this court receives any corroboration from an unbiased source, this judgment stands."

Deflated, Matt swayed, and caught himself on the table on his palms, despite the shooting pain up his right arm. God Damn it. He'd known it was coming. He had known the case was slim, but that had not stopped him praying.

Rumbles of congratulation arose from Lee's side of the courtroom, while Matt's handful of supporters groaned in sympathy—most of the people he knew couldn't take time off work just to sit around here all day, but a few of the shipyards' wealthier members occupied the benches at his back.

The judge banged his gavel. "However, the bench would like to issue a strong reprimand against the defendant, Charles Lee. During these proceedings, many prejudicial statements were made regarding both Mr. Percy and his crew, in spite of a total lack of evidence of any wrong-doing. The worst of which Mr. Percy may be accused is the failure to follow established custom in securing fresh trading partners. A mistake I daresay he shall not repeat." His watery gaze fell at last upon Matt, his face creased in an understanding expression.

Matt forced himself to stand erect. "Thank you, Your Honor."

"Indeed, Your Honor," Lee echoed. "Thank you."

Judge Cooper rose and stalked away as if the proceedings wearied him, as well they might.

"We did our best. Sorry it didn't turn out in our favor," Joseph said, and put out his hand.

"Thanks for all your work." Matt managed to shake his hand, though it left his arm still feeling weak. He took up Will's cap and stared at the plain brim. No luck there. Joseph scooped his papers together and pushed them into a leather satchel. As the audience broke up into knots of conversation, Matt started up the aisle. He nodded to Roger Minott as his benefactor stepped by to say a few words to his brother-in-law, Joseph. Ahead, Janiri descended the stairs and stood by the door, bouncing Clara gently against her shoulder. The baby squealed and stretched out her arms as Matt approached, and he took her against him, feeling her shift from hot to cool as she snuggled into him, perched on his left arm.

"Matt!" Roger called, returning up the aisle. "Let me walk you out—better yet, take my carriage back to town. There's room for all of us." He nodded to Janiri and gestured for her to precede them. From the shifting shade of her eyes, Matt could see the blaze building within her. "Truly, come. At the least, you deserve to get home in comfort. Surely with the baby?" His smile came and went.

Janiri flashed Matt a look, and he raised his eyebrows at her, tipping his head toward Roger. Now, more than ever, he needed to keep friendly with everyone he could—especially anyone who might be in a position to one day get him back aboard a ship. "Thanks. We'd be pleased to accept. Besides, Clara would love that." To this, Janiri could only sigh her agreement.

One of the Minott coachmen waited outside, hurrying to bring up the carriage when they emerged from the building into the waning day. Lee and his associates piled into a huge Concord Coach and set out down the Meadows road toward Phippsburg. Matt tore his eyes from the coach and watched as Roger's smaller carriage arrived. The coachman helped Janiri up into the carriage, and Matt passed over Clara as he climbed in beside her.

Roger settled on the cushion opposite. "Rotten verdict."

The conveyance barely gave room for their knees, but was still finer than anything Matt would ever have. "I'm sure Old Man Lee would disagree."

"Old Man Lee is a snake," said Janiri, holding the baby to look out the window.

Adjusting his posture to give her more space, Roger chuckled uncomfortably. "You have the right of that. I heard some of the talk—I gather he's already got plans for the gold now that he's not legally bound to hold it aside."

Matt winced.

"Sorry." Roger watched out the window for a time as they rolled past the houses of Bath, then the shipyards that began where the land narrowed into Phippsburg. Low tide left wide mudflats where shorebirds picked their way along, searching for treasure. "Look, Matt. I don't want to be a carrion crow here, but there is something." Roger stopped, waiting for Matt's nod. "I know you need to think ahead, toward the coming seasons. I'm glad to see your arm's recovering, but…"

Leaning back into his corner, Matt regarded the other man and tried to brace for whatever came next. "What is it you want to say, Roger?"

"I wondered if you might be looking to sell your house." Roger put up his hands immediately as Matt recoiled. "I'm not saying you are, just that's your most obvious asset. It has value, and you might need the money. Emily's been talking about building or moving, now that our own family's growing, and your house is a right lovely place, Matthew. You know I'd treat you fairly. Might be, you could buy one of the smaller places near the yard."

Janiri swung about from the window, drawing a cry of protest from Clara. "Matthew's family built that house, sir. He and his sisters were born there. Of course he has no desire to move."

"Desire might not be the whole of it, Janiri." Matt watched the boughs of maple slide overhead, then the end of Parker's Head Pond came into view. "I'll think about it. Could you let me out here? Will planned to ask the foreman today if they might have a place for me at the mills. I'd be obliged if you'd take Janiri—"

"No. We'll walk with you. Come, Clara." Janiri gathered the baby close again.

Roger rapped on the ceiling, and the coachman drew to a halt.

"I appreciate the ride, Roger, and, everything. I'll think about the house." Matt shook Roger's hand, then stood aside and watched as the two horses turned smartly down the road toward the Minott estate. Janiri let out a hiss. Matt turned, ready to chastise her for thinking ill of someone who only meant them good—then he saw why she was hissing. Lee's coach jaunted down the long road toward the head where the sawmill dam crossed the pond.

"What is he doing here?"

"I have told you, he is a snake—no, not a snake. They can devour only one thing at a time while he is rapacious."

Dust from the coach's passing muddied the air, and Clara gave a little cough. Matt waved away the dust. "No good dwelling on the past."

"After all, you are the king of next week, not this one." The ruffles at her bodice fluttered in the wind off the river and her hair rippled more slowly in the rising heat of her own body. "Does it not make you angry? Why don't you fight him?"

"I did fight him, in court. That's how it's done in a civilized country. I fought him, I lost." He flung up his hands. "Why? Because your father wouldn't give me a contract. A simple piece of paper that seemed so insignificant at the time."

"Because it is. Anyone can see you completed your contract."

"And anyone can see that something was wrong with the deal. It's not just the paper, it's the entire expedition. Gold with markings nobody can identify from an island no one can find. Men who have little recollection of where they were or what they did there—who brought home no souvenirs: no carvings, no beads, no dresses for their wives. The judge is right—there is no evidence that your nation even exists! I'm the only one who knows the truth and I've sworn never to reveal it at the risk of losing my wife, the only good thing that came out of my one command." The fury of his own voice surprised him. So much of this past year had been focused on this day, on the moment he was redeemed by the law only to have it capsize beneath him. Instead, he found himself sinking, clawing the mud of his life just to try to stay above water.

"Then wish for it. The evidence, if that is the little thing that will make everything right again."

"That's exactly my point. I can't produce a contract now, when I've not had one for all this time. What, should I wish to have your island added to the sea charts when everyone knows it wasn't there yesterday?" He clasped her shoulders, looking into her eyes where the fire burned. "Janiri, I know that, to you, magic is the answer. It keeps us warm, it keeps us fed. You can use it to travel whenever you want, wherever you want. But in my world, every little thing is bound to everything else. This community, it survives because of those bonds: sailors becoming ice men, neighbors feeding each other, offering each other the help they need."

"Then there is Lee, the snake who wishes everyone here to believe you are a criminal. If you will not wish for your evidence, you might at least wish for vengeance!"

Clara whimpered, and her mouth worked toward an all-out wail. Janiri bounced a little up and down, side to side, and the baby settled in spite of her mother's distraction.

"Vengeance. That's a different kind of bond. That's like the rebels clinging to their old ways, willing to die for a thing that should never have been. A man can't be bound to the past when the world has moved on." In spite of his bold words, he couldn't deny that it hurt. "Face it, Janiri, I lost. The world is moving on."

"Then perhaps we should be moving on. To another place where Lee's poison won't find you."

Sell the house his grandfather built. Give up forever the dream of having his own ship, the legacy he wanted to offer his daughter. Janiri lived between the worlds, how could she understand what this place meant to him, these people living and working together.

She stepped closer to him, their heads pressed together, and said, "Come back to my world, Matthew Percy. Come where the magic is everything."

A land without ice or snow, without toil or heartache, where nobody climbed March Hill or fell in the trying. A world without pine trees and maples. A world of uncalloused hands. A world without ships. "I don't think I could live in your country," he whispered.

Her heat flared. "I am not sure I wish to live in yours. Not if it can destroy you for want of a page."

Matt found that he had no answer. His throat felt too tight for speech as if he breathed in her fire, and his chest burned. What were the wishes for if not to save himself when there was no other recourse? He took her hand over his elbow, and they walked, silently simmering, along the aisle of maple trees beside the mill pond. Four mills occupied the dam at the far end, the whine of the saws growing in the air and the whiff of sawdust always hanging over them. Heaps of cut planks lay golden in the sunshine as men carried more to add to the stacks. And there, among it all, sat Lee's coach, with Lee himself standing outside, talking with one of the owners. "You should go on home. I'll find Will and see what he says."

Janiri stood, her gaze caught on Lee. As if her eyes drew his attention—and well they might—Lee glanced in their direction. His brow furrowed, then his lips parted to show his teeth. "Matthew Percy! Ah, yes, you should be here. Come, come over."

"Don't go," she whispered.

"I have to live here, and I don't expect he's moving any time soon."

"No, you do not," she said, her words stinging his cheek, but he kissed her briefly and straightened Will's cap on his head before he marched over.

"Good afternoon, Mr. Lee. I thought you might be off for a celebratory drink."

"Oh, but I am celebrating. I have some ready cash for investing, and I've a contract for buying up the mills." Lee spread his arms expansively. "It is a fine concession, don't you think? And—I owe this thought to you, actually—" his smile looked horribly genuine—"The Parker's Head Pond would be an excellent ice pond, don't you agree? With my ships and a good supply of ice, plus the sawdust to pack it in, I think Lee industries could do quite well."

Matt reeled. "You're using the money I earned to build the trade that I thought of?"

Lee patted his pockets, then came up with something between his fingers. "An excellent point, my boy. You deserve a little something for the inspiration." He flipped Matt a golden coin that winked in the sunlight.

It tumbled through the air of late summer, hot as flame and red with sunset. Matt's right shoulder ached.

He sucked in a breath, his fist already balled. As the coin struck the ground, Matt swung hard and fast, ending in a solid impact. Lee's nose crunched beneath his fist, blood spurting.

Lee staggered back with a yelp, hands clasped over his face.

"I wish you knew—" Matt shouted, his fists shaking. He could feel the fire at his back and the churning power that swelled through him, waiting.

"What? What should I know?" Lee waved away the mill owner's aid in favor of his own handkerchief pressed to staunch the blood though it muffled his voice. "I am now confirmed that you are a criminal and a miscreant and deserve to be jailed on charges of assault."

"What should you know?" Matt echoed. "What it feels like to lose. To work your whole goddamned life for something only to have some bastard steal it from you. To reach and scrape and struggle and be left with nothing, with less than what you started with. To be taken on as a partner, only to be abandoned at the first chance. For what? For money, Lee, is that all you care about? Because my crew weren't your crew, but my own? Do you know how many men would have testified if the court had let them? Every goddamned one! Every one: black and white and every shade between. How many men would stand up for you without your money?" Matt kicked the coin away. It rolled in the dirt and fell with a puff of sawdust. "You want me arrested? Fuck you, Charles Lee. I'd rather rot in prison than work in any mill of yours, not when you've bought it with the money I earned."

He executed a military pivot and walked away. The sensation of power building drained away, but he felt no weaker for it. If anything he walked taller than he had for many a month, shaking out his right hand, a few flecks of Lee's blood falling away as he came back to Janiri and grinned. "Well, now we'll really have to move."

Janiri's eyes burned. "But you did not finish the wish! Couldn't you feel it? I could." Her hand thumped her chest and Clara let out a wail. "I could feel it waiting, your desire calling to my power. Why didn't you finish?"

Clara's arms waved, and Matt caught her up and let her curl against his chest as he walked away, taking their voices beyond the millyard. "Because it wouldn't be right. Because I fought a war for men's freedom, even if that means the freedom to be a bastard."

"He made you suffer. He offered the coin only to make it worse."

"Do you think I don't know that?"

"I cannot believe you will simply let him go, not like this."

"I didn't let him go. I think I broke his nose."

"Matthew Percy—you let me believe that your people are strong and proud. Perhaps you lack the djinn's fire, but that men of the earth have their own strength."

"The strength of fire is in what it burns. The strength of the earth is in what it builds." He glanced back to the cluster of men around Lee trying to placate him. The millworkers stood at a distance, some watching Lee, others watching Matt walk away. Will squatted down where the coin had fallen and rose again, leaving it where it lay as the men drifted back to work. "Lee's not worth it. He's not worth my last wish." Matt put on a smile and looked down into Clara's eyes. The swirl of djinn fire faded back to a pale green, and his smile didn't feel so false any more. "How's my beautiful girl?"

"Not worth a wish? Perhaps you are right." Janiri's voice sounded strange, tight and hard. "I should like a moment's privacy."

To flame with her passion, no doubt. It touched him that she cared so much about his own reputation. From the rise where they stood, he saw the channel of the Kennebec River, where a proud ship sailed home, and his heart fell. Not only a full-rigged vessel, dropping her sails as they came into port, but the ship was Lee-built. Every ship now passing the point would pierce him like an arrow, Lee-built or not. Matt couldn't bear the thought of watching, day in, day out, as every ship left without him. He turned away. "Let's go home, Clara." They had packing to do.

Matt started up the bluff and turned toward home, crooning to his daughter as they walked. Up ahead, beyond the smaller white houses, stood the pretty blue house on the hill, its white trim gilded by the late afternoon sun. The house where his father was born, the house where his mother had died. Roger's family would love the place as much as he did. After a while, at his back, he felt the fires of Janiri's anger on his behalf. It warmed him to know she cared so much, that his grief was shared, even if she did not understand his restraint. By the time they reached the door, the glow of sunset reflected bright in his windows. Matt shifted Clara to his other hip and raised the latch, his hand lingering on the worn iron fitting, made by a local smith decades ago, when they barely even had a country.

Shouts rang in the distance, against a rising sound like the wind through dry leaves. Matt's head rose, then he spun about. The light on his windows was not the sun, nor was it Janiri's presence that warmed his back. Down below, smoke billowed into the sky and flames danced in the millyard. They spread from heaps of lumber though mounds of sawdust, rushing along the top of the dam from one building to the next, a great unholy conflagration of crimson bounding toward the sky. Sinuous arms of flame waved from the rooftops, and men screamed and fled. Some of them leapt into the pond on the one side, or the river on the other. Lee's great coach rocked as the horses spooked, then they were running, galloping back down the road.

"Janiri!" Matt shouted, scanning the ground between the house and the mills. "Janiri!" She did not appear. He cradled Clara's head against his chest and started running himself. What could he do? What could anyone do? The fire spread too fast. In moments, it would leap the lumber to the trees, to the houses. By supper time, all of Parker's Head could lie in ruin.

Hot ashes blew into his face as he ran for the street. Clara started crying, her little hands gripped in his jacket, and he cradled her head with his own rough hand. "Janiri!" Matt spun a circle. She said she would always hear him call. It did not mean she would always answer. But there was one thing to which she must reply.

Matt planted his feet, facing the roaring fire and the chaos of men surrounding it. "I wish—" he began, and felt as if the blaze rushed through him in that moment, burning in his chest with the power.

A hand pressed over his mouth, an arm of flame crackling to a shoulder, to a figure who burned to life even as he stared, his eyes watering from the heat. A gown of scorching red rushed into being. A crown of golden sparks lit her face and dark shadows swirled down over her shoulders. Her other hand caught the back of his head—not burning, not yet, though his nostrils tingled with the rising heat.

"This is what I am," she said, her voice a wind in his ears. "Will you not let me be this? Let me do this? For you."

His eyeballs felt dry, his throat parched beneath the clasp of her hand. Gently, he shook his head. He reached up, trying to lift her hand away. Flames shot forth, singeing his hand and he jerked it back.

Stalking toward him, keeping his mouth shut, she forced him off the road, taking the lead in this silent dance. He stumbled, his back pressed against an oak, his heart thundering. Tahari's every warning rang through his memory, and the image of Crowley's corpse haunted his eyes.

"He deserves nothing. Even you want this for him, for him to lose," she hissed. "To know what it is to suffer! I am giving what you want."

In spite of her fearsome strength, she remained his wife, the mother of his child. Keeping her gaze, he shook his head. Again, he reached for her hand, sliding his fingers over hers, prying away her grip, and she let him though her hand burned with fury. "I wish the fire were out," he said hoarsely. The power coursed through him in a tidal wave, the union of his desire and her spark.

"Why?" She howled in the wind. "Why can you not revel in your enemy's defeat?"

"Why should I wish for any man to hurt as I do? Besides it's not Lee you're hurting, it's the hundred men who work the mills who need to feed their families. Will is down there, Janiri, so are half my sailors! I told you, the strength of earth is what it builds: the mills, the ships, the town, the whole of this damnable country, they weren't built just for the rich, for the men who own them. We are all a part of it, and when it burns, we all burn with it." He gasped for breath, his lungs seared by the heat from without, and the pressure of the wish that built within. "Release the wish, Janiri. If ever you loved me, let it go."

She cried aloud, a piercing sound laced with words that burned. The magic poured from them both and left them breathless. Clara cooed with delight.

Beyond Janiri, the surface of the river rushed with all the strength of a full moon's tide. A swell surged above the water and crashed against the burning dam, water spraying, steaming, then subsiding into an uneasy sea. The fire sank down, its dance dying into nothing but smoke and embers. Janiri's crown of gold flickered and died. The flames that formed her spiraled deeper, draining away and leaving her skin unmarked, for once without its undertones of red. Her eyes remained dark and hollow, empty of fire. One of Clara's hands released Matt's jacket and tangled in Janiri's hair. Matt still gripped her hand, the other hand at the back of his neck, its touch transformed from strength to tenderness as she sifted her fingers through his hair. His heart pounded, and he felt as if not an ounce of water remained in him. He had been sucked dry by her power.

"If ever I loved you," she whispered. "As if I could cease to love you. You asked me to come with you, Matthew Percy, and to be your wife. I cannot. Forgive me." She pressed her mouth to his, her tongue stroking his scorched lips. "Forgive me," she said again, and her fingers slipped free of his hair.

Matt kept her hand, cupping it against his face. "You're leaving."

"I told you I could not stay forever. But I have loved being your wife, for as long as I was able." Her glance dipped to the child between them, still clinging to them both. "You are the builder; I can only burn."

"What about Clara?"

"You will build a life for both of you—I believe this, though I do not know how."

He managed half a smile. " I'll work it out," he told her. "Maybe next week."

She kissed him again, light and hot, then kissed their baby more tenderly. She untangled her hair from the tiny fingers, drawing it over her shoulder. Finally, she turned away, her long legs striding down the road toward the sea.

"Matt! Are you alright?" Will ran up the bank, panting, his clothes streaked with soot.

Matt pushed off from the tree and walked to meet him. "I'm fine—are you? I saw the flames."

"It looked as if—" Will shook his head, bracing his hands on his knees for a moment as he caught his breath. "Looked as if you caught fire."

"It was Janiri, she—"he glanced after her. Did it

matter now, now that she was leaving? "Tahari was right about the people of the island. They're not like us. They're djinn, genies."

Will straightened, his brow furrowed as he followed Matt's gaze. "Sweet Jesus, Matt, is that what you been hiding all this time?"

Matt nodded, swallowed hard. "I hated keeping it—"

"Shut up, Matt, I know that. But the gold?"

"Real enough. Her people are made of fire, Will, that's why they wouldn't write a contract."

"Sweet Jesus," Will said again. "They can grant wishes?"

"Only three." He tipped his head toward the ruined mills. "I just used my last one, putting out the fire. She thought I'd be pleased she made it happen, to get back at Lee."

"Now you're just, what, letting her go?"

"What am I supposed to do, Will? I can't hold fire in my hands for all that I've been trying."

"Little piece of it, maybe," Will said, gesturing toward Clara. She squealed and reached back for him. His eyes glazed with tears in an instant, and he pulled back. "Don't let it end that way, Matt—you wishing away what she's done for you, her just walkin' away."

"She has to go. When she's here, she's like a prisoner—she can't be who she is, not really. For the same reason, I can't go with her."

The wind carried a dash of the ocean's spray as Will stared into the distance, somewhere beyond Matt's face. "I had a wife, Matt. I was married, down south. Baby, too." He scrubbed the back of his wrist over his eyes. "We meant to get free together, but they set the dogs out, and we split up, hoping one of us would make it. Meet me by the old fence, I told her, where the barbed wire grows into the trees. Past the swamps, it was. I figured we'd make it that far. But don't you wait too long. By sun rise, you get out of there." He jabbed an urgent finger toward the memory. "I had to go to ground. Some folks took me in that night, got me out the next day. That's when I heard." He pressed his lips together. "She waited all night, and they found her by dawn, took her back, her and the baby both." He took a shuddering breath, and reached into his breast pocket to pull out that bit of faded gingham. "That's all I've got left of her. The master sold her down the river in case I tried to get her back. Looked for her after the war, couldn't find no trace."

"That's why it took you three months to follow me up here," Matt breathed. "Oh, Will." He gripped his friend's shoulder. "If I had a wish left, by God, I'd give it to you."

Tears tracked Will's face, and he fiercely wiped them away. "If she ain't gone yet, Matt, you go after her. One last kiss, one dance, I don't know what, but I would've given anything for one little moment with my Betsy." Together, they looked down the road toward the beach and the distant figure by the water. "Here, gimme that baby." Will took Clara in his arms with the ease of practice—something Matt should have noticed before. He plucked the borrowed cap from his head and clapped it on Will's.

From the yard far below, he heard someone calling his name. Damn—had Lee really called the constables? He stripped off his heavy jacket and tossed it aside.

"Whoever it is, tell 'em I'll be back—tell 'em I just had to say good-bye."

"Go, Matt, go!"

Matt was already running for all he was worth. His feet pounded the packed earth of the road, the maple leaves shaking as he ran by, skidding down the slope, then over the grass of the Widow Stinson's yard. He leapt the low granite ledge, and struck the rocky sand below, fingers spread against it as he absorbed the jump. "Janiri—don't leave yet."

A shadow flickered by the water, and he thought he saw it turn. Dusting off his hands, Matt strolled down as her face came clear, then she emerged as if she walked from behind a veil.

"I cannot stay," she said as he clasped her in his arms. "Even if you wished it."

"I know. I won't ask." He kissed her then, her hair sliding down over his arms, drawing her close in so that every inch of him could feel her, as if she were the fire and he had once more fallen through the ice. Her hands roved over his back, down to his waist, up to play, once more, with his hair, freeing it from the ribbon to catch between her fingers. He buried his face against her shoulder, breathing in the scent of her, the spice, the warmth. She was the hearth he wished he could always come home to. He wished…

Matt lifted his head, her face so very close to his. "I still have another wish, don't I. That first time, I wished for you to be my wife, but I didn't feel anything." He laughed and shook his head. "Oh, I felt a lot of things, but not that, not the spark of magic."

Her eyes glowed, and she laughed as well, her deft

fingers stroking back an escaped tendril of his hair. "I told you you need not wish for that, but you never heard."

"Because I'd never wished for anything so fervently in all my life. You were never going to tell me."

"These wishes are the pact of my people. We go to lengths not to give them, we twist the words and meanings, we see the curses and we fail to share them. You asked what holds my people together as charity holds yours, and it is this." Her face softened, almost wistful, almost human. "It was to be the story I could tell my father when I finally went home, the day a captain wished for me, and I tricked him and kept his first wish. His last wish." She gazed into his eyes. "Did you want to make it, is that why you followed?"

"I might," he answered, thinking of Will. "But there's a few things I want to try first."

Her laughter flowed around him, the way it had that first night. "Of course there are."

"I didn't come after you for the wishes." He shifted his hands, one to her waist, one held high, waiting for hers. "One last dance?"

She slipped her hand into his, the other on his arm. He stepped into a waltz, and she followed, graceful on the sand as he danced the pattern and she gazed into his face, her eyes alight. Her ruffled skirts flared out as she turned and her hair stroked over his fingers. Faint whistling floated on the breeze, and footsteps approached, but slowly as they danced. She needed to go home, to be free, and he needed to face whatever came next.

He spun her out, then drew her back in, close to him.

"You'll always hear me when I call?"

"I may not always answer." She brushed a kiss on his cheek. "Who knows? I might have another captain." A tiny drop of flame slid from the corner of her eye like a falling star. "But never one so bold."

The whistling grew into a tune, and Janiri stiffened, but Matt whispered, "He knows," and she relaxed into his arms for one last turn, one last movement, one last embrace. She faded from his arms in a wisp of smoke and a breath of heat that flared across his lips, then she was gone, and Matt let his arms fall, empty.

Union cap perched on his head, Will sat on the granite ledge, feet dangling, Clara sleeping in the crook of his arm. He held out a stiff paper. A warrant? He twitched the paper as Matt hesitated, then Matt released the past and moved on. He stepped up to the stone. "What is that?"

"Not what you think. Tripp's working at the docks as a stevedore; he brought it over soon's it made landfall. Take a look."

Matt took the paper and turned it over. A photograph. It showed an empty beach with a tall cliff to one side and a fringe of forest beginning at the edge of the picture. In the foreground stood a cross, carefully carved by a shipwright's skill. *RIP John Crowley, Phippsburg, Maine.* Crowley's grave. On the shore of an uncharted island.

"Tahari came through—took the commission to pilot Lee's expedition. That bird-watcher they brought along, he took photos of everything." Will's teeth flashed white. "That ain't the best part, though." He lifted up his cap, revealing a second one underneath, this one battered, stained, the gold braid still caught around the crown, a withered brown maple leaf tucked into the band.

"But that's impossible!" Matt snatched his cap and studied it, then he spun about toward the empty shore.

"Maybe so," Will agreed. "But everybody knows it's yours. That bird-watcher's got pictures of it, too, next to the remains of one helluva party. And a few maple leaves, like you might find at the bottom of some Center Pond ice. Copies already on the way to the newspaper, the courthouse, the shipyards..."

Slowly, Matt placed the cap back on his head and stared at the photo, the proof he needed that his story, however strange, was true. A fair share, plus damages. He, too, was grinning. "What do you say, Will, you fancy a steamship this time? We can take the southern route. Come springtime, that Parker Head ice is going places." He gazed up at the shore where the river met the sea. "Maybe something with a low draft. Something that can ply up the rivers."

Will blew out a breath. "You dreamer."

"Yes, sir." And if need be, he kept one last wish in his breast pocket. If the strength of men couldn't find what they were seeking, the magic of the Djinn would serve. Down on the beach, something gleamed rosy in the sand, a set of footprints in glass, forming the pattern of a dance, her steps cast in fire on the Phippsburg shore.

THE END

About the Author

E. C. Ambrose writes knowledge-inspired adventure fiction including *The Dark Apostle* series about medieval surgery, *The Singer's Legacy* fantasy series as by Elaine Isaak, and the Bone Guard international thrillers as by E. Chris Ambrose, beginning with *The Mongol's Coffin*. In the process of researching her books, Elaine learned how to hunt with a falcon, clear a building of possible assailants, and pull traction on a broken limb. Her short stories have appeared in *Fireside*, *Warrior Women*, and *Fantasy for the Throne*, among many others, and she has edited several volumes of *New Hampshire Pulp Fiction*. Elaine has taught at the Odyssey Writing Workshop, as well as at conventions and writers' groups across the United States, and judged writing competitions from New Hampshire Literary Idol to the World Fantasy Award.

Elaine dropped out of art school to found her own business. A former professional costumer and soft sculpture creator, Elaine now works as a part-time adventure guide. In addition to writing, Elaine creates wearable art employing weaving, dyeing, and felting into her unique garments. To learn about all of her writing, check out RocinanteBooks.com

More great fantasy novellas from GUARDBRIDGE BOOKS.

Death by Effigy
Mystery, Magic, and Marionettes in 19th Century Burma.
by Karen L. Abrahamson
A traditional Burmese puppetry troupe is more than meets the eye: these puppets hold living spirits.

Aung, the troupe's elderly singer, must navigate the labyrinth of court intrigues to solve a mystery and appease angry spirits—goals which might might be at odds.

A Fledgeling Abiba
by Dilman Dila
An orphaned teenage girl tries to survive on her own and understand her magical powers while a sorcerous plague sweeps the country. She may hold the key to its cure, but what she really wants is somewhere she can call home and family.

The Madness of Pursuit
by Carmelo Rafala
Dema Ägan is a notorious pirate woman, who killed her former capitan, stole his ship, and plies the seas with her J'Niah witch companion, Rymah. Or so the legends say.

Myriad Lands
Anthology of Multi-cultural and Non-traditional fantasy.
Beyond familiar tropes, there is a world of possibilities for fantasy literature. This 2 volume anthology contains stories from around our world and breathtaking fictional worlds.

Features stories by Tade Thompson, Mary Anne Mohanraj, Phenderson Djèlí Clark, Tanith Lee, Adrian Tchaikovsky, Walter Dinjos, and more.

All are available at our website and online retailers.

http://guardbridgebooks.co.uk

CPSIA information can be obtained
at www.ICGtesting.com
Printed in the USA
JSHW021943270623
43888JS00003B/164

9 781911 486466